WHAT IS NEW WAVE SCIENCE FICTION?

WHAT IS THE NEW TOMORROWS?

THE NEW TOMORROWS is a predestined collision of fifteen first-rate stories of somewhat scientific speculative fiction, collected and commented on by Norman Spinrad, himself the author of the controversial novel

BUG JACK BARRON

"I submit them as proof positive that *something* has indeed been going on in the past decade. Leaving the labels and ideological epithets to the mandarins. I hope to give some feel for *what* has been going on, and let waves break where they may."

—Norman Spinrad

THE NEW
TOMORROWS

Edited by

NORMAN SPINRAD

BELMONT TOWER BOOKS • NEW YORK CITY

THE NEW TOMORROWS
A BELMONT/TOWER BOOK—1973

Published by

Belmont Tower Books
185 Madison Avenue
New York, N.Y. 10016

This book is dedicated to
PHILIP JOSÉ FARMER

THE NEW TOMORROWS

by Norman Spinrad

Science fiction is going through changes. That much, at least, seems beyond reasonable dispute. The science fiction written in 1971, taken as a whole, is a far different thing than the science fiction produced in 1961. The years 1965-1970 saw a great internal dispute within the science fiction genre over a poorly understood constellation of phenomena discussed under the broad general label of the New Wave.

Some of the ideological declarations that have been made concerning the New Wave have been as meaningless as they have been asinine. Proponents of so-called traditional science fiction have declared that the New Wave does not exist, while out of the other sides of their mouths attacking this supposedly nonexistent phenomenon as nihilistic, anti-rational, involuted, and a threat to the special virtues that supposedly distinguish science fiction from "mainstream." For their part, some of the writers and critics who have become associated with the label New Wave (whether willingly or not) have expended a great deal of energy in attempting to substitute the label "speculative fiction" for the label "science fiction" when classifying their own product. This enables them to use the tonier "speculative fiction" when promoting their work in polite company while retaining the magic letters "SF" on their bookcovers.

Most of the debate over the New Wave has been on this level. Idealistic people like Michael Moorcock have been attacked as cynics. Writers like Kurt Vonnegut, Jr., whose work is clearly speculative or science fiction but whose success has enabled him to escape the narrow confines of the science fiction ghetto are attacked by "science fiction professionals" as traitors to something-or-other. One science fiction writer of considerable genre repute has even suggested that any work not clearly labelled "science fiction" by its publisher be barred from consideration for the Nebula award given by the Science Fiction Writers of America. On the other hand, certain writers have gone to great extremes to publicly insist that novels of theirs which are science fiction by any sane definition are in fact something else.

It seems to me that most of this debate over the New Wave has been so much hot air. Clearly, something important has been going on the past decade, something with ramifications in the larger world of literature, and perhaps even beyond. To insist, as some people have, that all this is a "packaging phenomenon," a hype on the part of a few writers, editors, and publishers, borders on the schizoid. But just as clearly, the substitution of one set of arbitrary labels for another is not what it is all about.

This book, then, is not an attempt to continue the debate over the New Wave, nor is it an attempt to prove that the phenomenon does not exist. I am stuck with certain terms like "science fiction," "New Wave," "speculative fiction," and the like. To try to coin a new set of labels in order to avoid these terms would be as quixotic as pretending, as some people do, that these words are significant in and of themselves. What I hope to do here is explore the ongoing changes in science (speculative) fiction as it is written, read, influenced, and published, and to do this using examples from the works of some of the writers involved, examples that will be entertaining as well as enlightening. Some of the stories in this book are by authors familiar in traditional science fiction. Others are by writers who have grown up inside the genre, expanding its boundaries in the process. Some are by younger writers just starting out, others by writers who have been pursuing courses independent of science fiction but tangential to it.

What all these writers have in common is that they are now doing very much their own private things; if there is a label under which they may be all classified together, it is by accident, not by their own design. What the stories have in common is that they all contain speculative elements, that most of them were published as science or speculative fiction, that few of them could or would have been published as science fiction ten years ago, and that a good many of them might not have been written at all in the creative climate which prevailed in science fiction prior to the mid-sixties. I submit them as proof positive that *something* has indeed been going on in the past decade. Leaving the labels and ideological epithets to the mandarins, I hope to give some feel for *what* has been going on, and let the waves break where they may.

It is customary to begin discussions of modern speculative fiction with a definition of science fiction, usually either so broad as to be meaningless or so narrow as to be self-defeating. There is only one definition of science fiction that seems to make pragmatic sense: "Science fiction is anything published as science fiction."

Science fiction is a marketing definition, or at least it has been. There are at this writing seven magazines in the United States and one in England which call them-

11

selves "science fiction magazines." There are about a dozen publishers in the United States, most of them paperback houses, who publish regular lines of science fiction, that is, books which are labelled "science fiction" on their covers. In England, there are nearly a dozen hardcover houses with science fiction lines, and about as many paperback houses. In addition, a great deal of fantasy is published by the same houses and magazine publishers under labels such as "SF," "science fantasy," or "STF." This sort of fantasy is written for the most part by regular "science fiction" writers and is packaged and marketed with science fiction books and magazines.

With a few exceptions, publishers of science fiction novels, collections, and anthologies can count on a rather narrow range of sales for books published with the science fiction label. In the United States, few paperback science fiction books sell less than 30,000 copies or more than 75,000. Few hardcover science fiction books sell less than 1,000 copies or more than 5,000. Without benefit of significant advertising or promotion, a paperback publisher figures to average 40-60,000 sales on its science fiction books, a hardcover house 3-4,000. *Analog,* the best-selling science fiction magazine sells about 100,000 copies a month. The minimum monthly circulation for a science fiction magazine is about 30,000 copies; much less, and the magazine folds.

The pay rates of regular science fiction writers—that is, people who write primarily for the science fiction magazines and the science fiction lines of paperback and hardcover publishers—are similarly modest and narrow. For short fiction, wordage rates almost always apply. A professional science fiction writer can count on no less than 1¢ a word and no more than 5¢ a word for a short story, with most short fiction being paid for at 3-4¢ a word. Few paperback originals receive advances less than $1,500 or more than $3,000. Hardcover advances range between $1,000 and $4,000, with few exceptions. The author splits the paperback money with the hardcover publisher, and these reprint sales are seldom for less than $2,500 or more than $6,000. Significant payment of royalties above the advance to the author are rare; the publishers know pretty well how science fiction sells and adjust their advances and royalty rates accordingly.

Perhaps you're wondering why I've dwelt on the economics and publishing mechanics of the genre. Isn't this sort of thing more suitable to bull sessions among writers than to a discussion of science fiction as literature?

By now, Marshall McLuhan's dictum that "The medium is the message" has become a cliché. But I believe that it is impossible to understand the changes that have been going on within speculative fiction without realizing that traditionally the medium of science fiction publishing as a marketing, packaging, and economic phenomenon has had a dominant influence, indeed virtually a determining influence, on the development of science fiction as literature.

Keeping in mind the definition of science fiction as anything published as science fiction, the position taken by Kurt Vonnegut begins to make more sense. For the sake of clarity, I will use the term "science fiction" to mean anything published and labelled as science fiction and the term "speculative fiction" to mean any fiction which contains a speculative element, that is an element which belongs to the could-be-but-isn't. Thus, all science fiction is speculative fiction, but all speculative fiction isn't science fiction. Kurt Vonnegut, for example, writes speculative fiction: so do Philip K. Dick, James Blish, Larry Niven, and Poul Anderson. But unlike the others, Vonnegut is not a science fiction writer—his work is not published as science fiction. Because the work of people like Vonnegut and Bradbury is not published as science fiction, it reaches a much wider audience, and the writers in question have much heftier bank balances. Most writers want their work to be read as widely and as appreciatively as possible and few writers loathe money. Therefore speculative writers who are good enough to reach an audience wider than that of science fiction readers take pains to dissociate their work from the marketing label of science fiction.

This is part of the constellation of phenomena called the New Wave. In the minds of the general public, science fiction means monsters, spaceships, and low-grade pulp writing. In the minds of literary critics, science fiction means commercial hackwork churned out by writers who are not to be taken seriously. These judgments are half-truths that are rapidly becoming no truths at all—another aspect of the so-called New Wave.

But why has science fiction come to be held in such low repute in the first place? Largely because science fiction has indeed been a marketing rather than a literary category, a commercial genre like westerns, mysteries, true confessions, or nurse novels. Books and magazines receive lurid and tasteless covers which exist solely to make the product instantly identifiable as science fiction. Since the publishers feel that the market for science fiction is static, modest, and consistent from book to book, they see no point in promoting or advertising science fiction. Further, since publishers seem to feel that there is a market for about two hundred science fiction books a year, Sturgeon's Law operates with a vengeance: 90 percent of the science fiction published is indeed crap.

Of course Sturgeon's Law states that 90 percent of *everything* is crap. Ninety percent of so-called mainstream fiction is crap. But the difference is that mainstream books are published and promoted on their own merits, since their sales from book to book are wildly inconsistent. However, since science fiction as a label automatically guarantees a fairly predictable sale, the crap and the fine books receive equal treatment. The novels of Philip K. Dick, Brian W. Aldiss, Theodore

14

Sturgeon, and other speculative writers whose work can stand in any literary company are buried in the dross.

To a large extent, the New Wave has simply been the recognition of these facts of life by a whole generation of writers. In the early sixties, a dozen or more speculative writers emerged who wrote speculative fiction for their own private and diverse literary reasons. They found themselves confronted by the commercial demands of science fiction publishing and the science fiction label. The publishers had some very firm opinions as to the typical consumer of their product: he was an adolescent male who wanted upbeat stories with plenty of action, told in straightforward conventional prose, and possessed of a set of parents who would frown on any sexuality in his reading matter.

Since these new writers were not really interested in turning out pulp stories for adolescents but were interested in exploring the literary possibilities of speculative fiction; since mainstream publishers still shunned their work as science fiction; and since they wanted their work published, conflict inevitably arose.

The writers were not only far ahead of the publishers in their literary adventurousness, they had a better picture of who their potential readers were and, since they were much closer to their own adolescence than the editors and publishers, had a far less patronizing opinion of the tastes of intelligent young people.

In England, Michael Moorcock, one of these new young writers, took over the pulp science fiction magazine *New Worlds* and gradually transformed it into an openly writer-oriented experimental magazine dedicated more to providing an arena for the literary development of speculative fiction than to showing a profit. The magazine never made money, and the writers were paid little or nothing; by dropping out of commercial science fiction publishing, *New Worlds* and its contributors encouraged the literary development of some of the best of the new generation of writers, such as Ballard, Sallis,

15

Disch, Jones, Sladek, Harrison, and half a dozen others. Previously, such writers would have either given up writing speculative fiction or been slowly forced by commercial and ego pressures into conventional science fiction modes.

Gradually, the new freedom in content, style, and form began to percolate upward into the publishing houses, first in Britain, then in the United States. Editors with more sophisticated tastes, wider backgrounds, and less cynicism penetrated the previously sealed-off area of science fiction publishing. Slowly, it became easier to publish speculative novels with explicit sexuality, psychological depth, unconventional style or form. Although this evolution has yet to transform magazine science fiction in the United States, outlets for similarly adventurous short speculative fiction have begun to open up in the form of books of original stories.

Since the majority of professional science fiction writers simply were not capable of writing on a serious literary level; since most science fiction editors and publishing executives were firmly wedded to the principles of science fiction as commercial pulp literature; and since "science fiction fans" were by and large a tradition-minded group not seriously concerned with genuine literary values, the inevitable reaction occurred, and the New Wave controversy was born.

Because some of the new speculative fiction deals explicitly with sex and reproduced human speech as it actually occurs, the New Wave was attacked as "depraved." Because some of the new speculative fiction is written in unconventional prose or couched in unfamiliar forms, the New Wave was categorically condemned as "obscure," "involuted," and "self-indulgent." Because some of the new speculative fiction eschews the mandatory happy endings of commercial science fiction or the uncritical acceptance of scientific advance as an absolute good, all of it was attacked as "downbeat," "pessimistic," and "anti-scientific" or even "anti-ration-

16

al." Because the new speculative fiction utilized a wide range of protagonists in whom good and evil mingled in many combinations as it does in us all, rather than confining itself to the heroic figures of traditional science fiction, it was categorically condemned as "anti-heroic," "anti-romantic," and "nihilistic."

What was actually being condemned, of course, was diversity. In the sense of a school of writing with rules of form, prose, content, or ideology, the New Wave does not exist. However, the traditionalist school of commercial science fiction does have some general rules regarding prose, form, content, and to some extent ideology. Since the essence of New Wave is the disregard of the rules of commercial science fiction, and since those thoroughly committed to a school of literature seldom recognize its limiting parameters for what they are, the diversity of the new speculative fiction was erroneously seen by the traditionalists as an ideology in itself, since such diversity clearly defied most of their shibboleths.

My own novel, *Bug Jack Barron,* was condemned as anti-heroic, anti-romantic, and pessimistic, even nihilistic. Whatever the merits of the book, any intelligent unbiased reader would have to realize that the point of view was in fact optimistic, that the protagonist was a "hero" in the classical sense, that the book was written very much in a romantic tradition, that it was not nihilistic at all. But the prose was experimental, and the sexuality and language explicit, which automatically identified the novel as New Wave. Thus all the totally invalid descriptions of the book arose not from judgement of the book itself, but from a Pavlovian response to the label. Similar things have happened in different ways to works of Philip José Farmer, Thomas M. Disch, J.G. Ballard, Michael Moorcock, and a host of others. Because a work of speculative fiction deviates from the traditional modes of science fiction in one or more aspects, some people automatically leap to the conclusion that it has all the attributes they erroneously attach to the New Wave.

Of all possible literary movements, a move toward the widest possible diversity in style, content, form, and philosophy will always be the hardest for traditionalists to grasp. I believe that this is what is occurring in speculative fiction today. I believe that the fifteen stories in this book will demonstrate that what the writers hold in common is dedication to private visions, rather than some imagined ideology or commonly held notion of prose style or form. Interestingly enough, several of the stories in this book are by writers who worked within the traditional parameters of science fiction for many years, and who have experienced an opening up in their work at mature stages in their careers.

What you are going to read is fifteen stories by fifteen individualists. If you expect a pattern to emerge, you will probably be disappointed. The only pattern here is a lack of pattern; the only stricture is freedom.

The only New Wave in speculative fiction is a wave of artistic diversity, and that is not a wave at all, but a timeless tide as primal as the soul of man.

Foreword to THE PLEASURE GARDEN OF
FELIPE SAGITTARIUS

It is fitting that *The New Tomorrows* begins with a story by Michael Moorcock, for if it is possible to single out one man as the key figure in the changes that began in speculative fiction in the sixties, Moorcock is that man. His editorship transformed the British science fiction magazine *New Worlds* into an open forum for experimentation, into the major research and development lab of modern speculative fiction. For many years, and at great personal cost, he kept the magazine afloat through censorship hassles and economic crises, without compromising its function as virtually the only truly adventurous outlet for short speculative fiction in the English language. Under his editorship, *New Worlds* encouraged the development of a whole generation of speculative writers and enabled older writers like Brian Aldiss and J.G. Ballard to publish work that would have found no outlet elsewhere. Still under thirty-five, Moorcock as an editor has already done more to open up the development of speculative fiction than any other editor in the checkered history of the field.

As a writer, Moorcock has led a strange double life. In one persona, he is perhaps the foremost living writer of "heroic fantasy," (sword & sorcery novels) a commercial category hardly noted for experimentation or literary excellence. Although he himself sometimes deprecates this aspect of his work, Moorcock's sword and sorcery stands above that of most writers in this field by dint of the obvious self-conscious knowledge of human

19

beings it displays and its resultant psychological depth. Moorcock plays the sword and sorcery game like visiting royalty.

Moorcock's more serious work bears a curious relationship to his heroic fantasy. Heroic fantasy uses myths and archetypes to manipulate the responses of the reader in a manner that is often unself-conscious even on the part of the writer himself. In his Jerry Cornelius novels (*The Final Programme, A Cure For Cancer*) and stories, Moorcock has carefully and deliberately created a synthetic modern archetype and mythology which he and other writers may then use as a mythic structure around which to blow stylistic, formal, and allusive riffs. Thus the Cornelius stories and novels, taken as a whole, are an exploration of the nature and genesis of myth and of the possible relationships of myth to literature.

In *Behold The Man,* Moorcock's novel about a Jesus-fixated neurotic who becomes the historical Jesus (which won a Nebula in its novelette version), he explores the relationship of myth and reality from an entirely different angle, combining psychological realism with a pleasantly nasty speculative imagination to produce a quite convincing portrait of Jesus-as-object-of-his-own-neurotic-fixation.

The story you are about to read, "The Pleasure Garden Of Felipe Sagittarius," defies any description or categorization. It too deals in a way with mythic processes, but in a way at right angles to anything else I have ever read. Here the speculative element lies not merely in the content but in the very concept itself. The levels in this story forever rebound and reverberate off each other. It is perhaps the best piece of short fiction Moorcock has written and one of the richest to be produced by the new speculative writers. Here Moorcock's explorations of the interrelation of myth and reality reach an ultimate which will be difficult to surpass.

THE PLEASURE GARDEN
OF FELIPE SAGITTARIUS
by Michael Moorcock

The air was still and warm, the sun bright and the sky blue above the ruins of Berlin as I clambered over piles of weed-covered brick and broken concrete on my way to investigate the murder of an unknown man in the garden of Police Chief Bismarck.

My name is Minos Aquilinas, top Metatemporal Investigator of Europe, and this job was going to be a tough one, I knew.

Don't ask me the location or the date. I never bother to find out things like that, they only confuse me. With me it's instinct, win or lose.

They'd given me all the information there was. The dead man had already had an autopsy. Nothing unusual about him except that he had paper lungs—disposable lungs. That pinned him down a little. The only place I knew of where they still used paper lungs was Rome. What was a Roman doing in Berlin? Why was he murdered in Police Chief Bismarck's garden? He'd been strangled, that I'd been told. It wasn't hard to strangle a man with paper lungs, it didn't take long. But who and why were harder questions to answer right then.

It was a long way across the ruins to Bismarck's place. Rubble stretched in all directions and only here and there could you see a landmark—what was left of the Reichstag, the Brandenburg Gate, the Brechtsmuseum and a few other places like that.

I stopped to lean on the only remaining wall of a

house, took off my jacket and loosened my tie, wiped my forehead and neck with my handkerchief and lit a cheroot. The wall gave me some shade and I felt a little cooler by the time I was ready to press on.

As I mounted a big heap of brick on which a lot of blue weeds grew I saw the Bismarck place ahead. Built of heavy, black-veined marble, in the kind of Valhalla/Olympus mixture they went in for, it was fronted by a smooth, green lawn and backed by a garden that was surrounded by such a high wall I only glimpsed the leaves of some of the foliage even though I was looking down on the place. The thick Grecian columns flanking the porch were topped by a baroque façade covered in bas-reliefs showing men in horned helmets killing dragons and one another apparently indiscriminately.

I picked my way down to the lawn and walked across it, then up some steps until I'd crossed to the front door. It was big and heavy, bronze I guessed, with more bas-reliefs, this time of clean-shaven characters in more ornate and complicated armour with two-handed swords and riding horses. Some had lances and axes, I noticed, as I pulled the bell and waited.

I had plenty of time to study the pictures before one of the doors swung open and an old man in a semi-military suit, holding himself straight by an effort, raised a white eyebrow at me.

I told him my name and he let me in to a cool, dark hall full of the same kinds of armor the men on the door had been wearing. He opened a door on the right and told me to wait. The room I was in was all iron and leather—weapons on the walls and leather-covered furniture on the carpet.

Thick velvet curtains were drawn back from the window and I stood looking out over the quiet ruins, smoked another stick, popped the butt in a green pot and put my jacket back on.

The old man came in again and I followed him out of that room, along the hall, up one flight of the wide stairs and in to a huge, less cluttered, room where I found the guy I'd come to see.

He stood in the middle of the carpet. He was wearing a heavily ornamented helmet with a spike on the top, a deep blue uniform covered in badges, gold and black epaulettes, shiny jackboots and steel spurs. He looked about seventy and very tough. He had bushy grey eyebrows and a big, carefully combed moustache. As I came in he grunted and one arm sprang into a horizontal position, pointing at me.

"Herr Aquilinas. I am Otto von Bismarck, Chief of Berlin's police."

I shook the hand. Actually it shook me, all over.

"Quite a turn up," I said. "A murder in the garden of the man who's supposed to prevent murders."

His face must have been paralyzed or something because it didn't move except when he spoke, and even then it didn't move much.

"Quite so," he said. "We were reluctant to call you in, of course. But I think this is your specialty."

"Maybe. Is the body still here?"

"In the kitchen. The autopsy was performed here. Paper lungs—you know about that?"

"I know. Now, if I've got it right, you heard nothing in the night—"

"Oh, yes, I did hear something—the barking of my wolfhounds. One of the servants investigated but found nothing."

"What time was this?"

"Time?"

"What did the clock say?"

"About two in the morning."

"When was the body found?"

"About ten—the gardener discovered it in the vine grove."

"Right—let's look at the body and then talk to the gardener."

He took me to the kitchen. One of the windows was

opened on to a lush garden, full of tall, brightly colored shrubs of every possible shade. An intoxicating scent came from the garden. It made me feel randy. I turned to look at the corpse lying on a scrubbed deal table covered in a sheet.

I pulled back the sheet. The body was naked. It looked old but strong, deeply tanned. The head was big and its most noticeable feature was the heavy black moustache. The body wasn't what it had been. First there were the marks of strangulation around the throat, as well as swelling on wrists, forearms and legs which seemed to indicate that the victim had also been tied up recently. The whole of the front of the torso had been opened for the autopsy and whoever had stitched it up again hadn't been too careful.

"What about clothes?" I asked the Police Chief.

Bismarck shook his head and pointed to a chair standing beside the table. "That was all we found."

There was a pair of neatly folded paper lungs, a bit the worse for wear. The trouble with disposable lungs was that while you never had to worry about smoking or any of the other causes of lung disease, the lungs had to be changed regularly. This was expensive, particularly in Rome where there was no State-controlled Lung Service as there had been in most of the European City-States until a few years before the war when the longer-lasting polythene lung had superseded the paper one. There was also a wrist-watch and a pair of red shoes with long, curling toes.

I picked up one of the shoes. Middle Eastern workmanship. I looked at the watch. It was heavy, old, tarnished and Russian. The strap was new, pigskin, with "Made in England" stamped on it.

"I see why they called us," I said.

"There *were* certain anachronisms," Bismarck admitted.

"This gardener who found him, can I talk to him?"

Bismarck went to the window and called: "Felipe!"

The foliage seemed to fold back of its own volition and a dark-haired young man came through it. He was tall, long-faced and pale. He held an elegant watering can in one hand. He was dressed in a dark green, high-collared shirt and matching trousers.

We looked at one another through the window.

"This is my gardener Felipe Sagittarius," Bismarck said.

Sagittarius bowed, his eyes amused. Bismarck didn't seem to notice.

"Can you let me see where you found the body?" I asked.

"Sure," said Sagittarius.

"I shall wait here," Bismarck told me as I went toward the kitchen door.

"OK." I stepped into the garden and let Sagittarius show me the way. Once again the shrubs seemed to part on their own.

The scent was still thick and erotic. Most of the plants had dark, fleshy leaves and flowers of deep reds, purples and blues. Here and there were clusters of heavy yellow and pink.

The grass I was walking on seemed to crawl under my feet and the weird shapes of the trunks and stems of the shrubs didn't make me feel like taking a snooze in that garden.

"This is all your work is it, Sagittarius?" I asked.

He nodded and kept walking.

"Original," I said. "Never seen one like it before."

Sagittarius turned then and pointed a thumb behind him. "This is the place."

We were standing in a little glade almost entirely surrounded by thick vines that curled about their trellises like snakes. On the far side of the glade I could see where some of the vines had been ripped and the trellis torn and I guessed there had been a fight. I still couldn't work out why the victim had been untied before the murderer strangled him—it must have been before, or else there wouldn't have been a fight. I checked the scene, but there were no clues. Through the place where the trellis was torn I saw a small summerhouse, built to represent a Chinese pavilion, all red, yellow and black lacquer with highlights picked out in gold. It didn't fit with the architecture of the house.

"What's that?" I asked the gardener.

"Nothing," he said sulkily, evidently sorry I'd seen it.

"I'll take a look at it anyway."

He shrugged but didn't offer to lead on. I moved between the trellises until I reached the pavilion. Sagittarius followed slowly. I took the short flight of wooden steps up to the veranda and tried the door. It opened. I walked in. There seemed to be only one room, a bedroom. The bed needed making and it looked as if two people had left it in a hurry. There was a pair of nylons tucked half under the pillow and a pair of man's underpants on the floor. The sheets were very white, the furnishings very oriental and rich.

Sagittarius was standing in the doorway.

"Your place?" I said.

"No." He sounded offended. "The Police Chief's."

I grinned.

Sagittarius burst into rhapsody. "The languorous scents, the very menace of the plants, the *heaviness* in the air of the garden, must surely stir the blood of even the most ancient man. This is the only place he can relax. This is what I'm employed for—why he gives me my head."

"Has this," I said, pointing to the bed, "anything to do with last night?"

"He was probably here when it happened, but I . . ." Sagittarius shook his head and I wondered if there was anything he'd meant to imply which I'd missed.

I saw something on the floor, stooped and picked it up. A pendant with the initials E.B. engraved on it in Gothic script.

"Who's E.B.?" I said.

26

"Only the garden interests me, Mr. Aquilinas—I do not know who she is."

I looked out at the weird garden. "Why does it interest you—what's all this for? You're not doing it to his orders, are you? You're doing it for yourself."

Sagittarius smiled bleakly. "You are astute." He waved an arm at the warm foliage that seemed more reptilian than plant and more mammalian, in its own way, than either. "You know what I see out there? I see deep-sea canyons where lost submarines cruise through a silence of twilit green, threatened by the waving tentacles of predators, half-fish, half-plant, and watched by the eyes of long-dead mermen whose blood went to feed their young; where squids and rays fight in a graceful dance of death, clouds of black ink merging with clouds of red blood, drifting to the surface, sipped at by sharks in passing, where they will be seen by mariners leaning over the rails of their ships; maddened, the mariners will fling themselves overboard to sail slowly toward those distant plant-creatures already feasting on the corpse of squid and ray. This is the world I can bring to the land—that is my ambition."

He stared at me, paused, and said: "My skull—*it's like a monstrous goldfish bowl!*"

I nipped back to the house to find Bismarck had returned to his room. He was sitting in a plush armchair, a hidden HiFi playing, of all things, a Ravel String Quartet.

"No Wagner?" I said and then: "Who's E.B.?"

"Later," he said. "My assistant will answer your questions for the moment. He should be waiting for you outside."

There was a car parked outside the house—a battered Volkswagen containing a neatly uniformed man of below average height, a small tooth-brush moustache, a stray lock of black hair falling over his forehead, black gloves on his hands which gripped a military cane in his lap. When he saw me come out he smiled, said "Aha," and got briskly from the car to shake my hand with a slight bow.

"Adolf Hitler," he said, "Captain of Uniformed Detectives in Precinct XII. Police Chief Bismarck has put me at your service."

"Glad to hear it. Do you know much about him?"

Hitler opened the car door for me and I got in. He went round the other side, slid into the driving seat.

"The chief?" He shook his head. "He is somewhat remote. I do not know him well—there are several ranks between us. Usually my orders came from him indirectly. This time he chose to see me himself and give me my orders."

"What were they, these orders?"

"Simply to help you in this investigation."

"There isn't much to investigate. You're completely loyal to your chief I take it?"

"Of course." Hitler seemed honestly puzzled. He started the car and we drove down the drive and out along a flat, white road, surmounted on both sides by great heaps of overgrown rubble.

"The murdered man had paper lungs, eh?" he said.

"Yes. Guess he must have come from Rome. He looked a bit like an Italian."

"Or a Jew, eh?"

"I don't think so. What made you think that?"

"The Russian watch, the Oriental shoes—the nose. That was a big nose he had. And they still have paper lungs in Moscow, you know."

His logic seemed a bit off-beat to me but I let it pass. We turned a corner and entered a residential section where a lot of buildings were still standing. I noticed that one of them had a bar in its cellar. "How about a drink?" I said.

"Here?" He seemed surprised, or maybe nervous.

"Why not?"

So he stopped the car and we went down the steps into the bar. A girl was singing. She was a plumpish brunette with a small, good voice. She was singing in English and I caught the chorus:

> *Nobody's grievin' for Steven,*
> *And Stevie ain't grievin' no more,*
> *For Steve took his life in a prison cell,*
> *And Johnny took a new whore.*

It was the latest hit in England. We ordered beers from the bartender. He seemed to know Hitler well because he laughed and slapped him on the shoulder and didn't charge us for the beer. Hitler seemed embarrassed.

"Who was that?" I asked.

"Oh, his name is Weill. I know him slightly."

"More than slightly, it looks like."

Hitler seemed unhappy and undid his uniform jacket, tilted his cap back on his head and tried unsuccessfully to push back the stray lock of hair. He looked a sad little man and I felt that maybe my habit of asking questions was out of line here. I drank my beer and watched the singer. Hitler kept his back to her but I noticed she kept looking at him.

"What do you know about this Sagittarius?" I asked.

Hitler shrugged. "Very little."

Weill turned up again behind the bar and asked us if we wanted more beer. We said we didn't.

"Sagittarius?" Weill spoke up brightly. "Are you talking about that crank?"

"He's a crank, is he?" I said.

"That's not fair, Kurt," Hitler said. "He's a brilliant man, a biologist—"

"Who was thrown out of his job because he was insane!"

"That is unkind, Kurt," Hitler said reprovingly. "He was investigating the potential sentience of plant life. A perfectly reasonable line of scientific inquiry."

From the corner of the room someone laughed

jeeringly. It was a shaggy-haired old man sitting by himself with a glass of schnapps on the little table in front of him.

Weill pointed at him. "Ask Albert. He knows about science."

Hitler pursed his lips and looked at the floor. "He's just an embittered old mathematics teacher—he's jealous of Felipe," he said quietly, so that the old man wouldn't hear.

"Who is he?" I asked Weill.

"Albert? A *really* brilliant man. He has never had the recognition he deserves. Do you want to meet him?"

But the shaggy man was leaving. He waved a hand at Hitler and Weill. "Kurt, Captain Hitler—good day."

"Good day, Doctor Einstein," muttered Hitler. He turned to me. "Where would you like to go now?"

"A tour of the places that sell jewellery, I guess," I said, fingering the pendant in my pocket, "I may be on the wrong track altogether, but it's the only track I can find at the moment."

We toured the jewellers. By nightfall we were nowhere nearer finding out who had owned the thing. I'd just have to get the truth out of Bismarck the next day, though I knew it wouldn't be easy. He wouldn't like answering my personal questions at all. Hitler dropped me off at the Precinct House where a cell had been converted into a bedroom for me.

I sat on the hard bed smoking and thinking. I was just about to get undressed and go to sleep when I started to think about the bar we'd been in earlier. I was sure someone there could help me. On impulse I left the cell and went out into the deserted street. It was still very hot and the sky was full of heavy clouds. Looked like a storm was due.

I got a cab back to the bar. It was still open.

Weill wasn't serving there now—he was playing the piano-accordion for the same girl singer I'd seen earlier. He nodded to me as I came in. I leaned on the bar and ordered a beer from the barman.

When the number was over Weill unstrapped his accordion and joined me. The girl followed him.

"Adolf not with you?" he said.

"He went home. He's a good friend of yours, is he?"

"Oh, we met years ago in Austria. He's a nice man, you know. He should never have become a policeman, he's too mild."

"That's the impression I got. Why did he ever join in the first place?"

Weill smiled and shook his head. He was a short, thin man, wearing heavy glasses. He had a large, sensitive mouth. "Sense of duty, perhaps. He has a great sense of duty. He is very religious, too—a devout Catholic. I think that weighs on him. You know these converts, they accept nothing, are torn by their consciences. I never yet met a happy Catholic convert."

"He seems to have a thing about Jews."

Weill frowned. "What sort of thing? I've never really noticed. Many of his friends are Jews. I am, and Sagittarius. . . ."

"Sagittarius is a friend of his?"

"Oh, more an acquaintance I should think. I've seen them together a couple of times."

It began to thunder outside. Then it started to rain.

Weill walked toward the door and began to pull down the blind. Through the noise of the storm I heard another sound, a strange, metallic grinding sound, a crunching sound.

"What's that?" I called. Weill shook his head and walked back towards the bar. The place was empty now. "I'm going to have a look," I said.

I went to the door, opened it, and climbed the steps.

Marching across the ruins, illuminated by rapid flashes of lightning like gunfire, I saw a gigantic metal monster, as big as a tall building. Supported on four telescopic legs, it lumbered at right angles to the street.

From its huge body and head the snouts of guns stuck out in all directions. Lightning sometimes struck it and it made an ear-shattering bell-like clang, paused to fire upward at the source of the lightning, and marched on.

I ran down the steps and flung open the door. Weill was tidying up the bar. I described what I'd seen.

"What is it, Weill?"

The short man shook his head. "I don't know. At a guess it is something Berlin's conquerors left behind."

"It looked as if it was made here . . ."

"Perhaps it was. After all, who conquered Berlin—?"

A woman screamed from a back room, high and brief.

Weill dropped a glass and ran towards the room. I followed. He opened the door. The room was homely. A table covered by a thick, dark cloth, laid with salt and pepper, knives and forks, a piano near the window, a girl lying on the floor.

"Eva!" Weill gasped, kneeling beside the body.

I gave the room another once over. Standing on a small coffee table was a plant. It looked at first rather like a cactus of unpleasantly mottled green, though the top curved so that it resembled a snake about to strike. An eyeless, noseless snake—with a mouth. There was a mouth. It opened as I approached. There were teeth in the mouth—or rather thorns arranged the way teeth are. One thorn seemed to be missing near the front. I backed away from the plant and inspected the corpse. I found the thorn in her wrist. I left it there.

"She is dead," Weill said softly, standing up and looking around. "How?"

"She was bitten by that poisonous plant," I said.

"Plant . . . ? I must call the police."

"That wouldn't be wise at this stage maybe," I said as I left. I knew where I was going.

Bismarck house—and the pleasure garden of Felipe Sagittarius.

It took me time to find a cab and I was soaked through when I did. I told the cabby to step on it.

I had the cab stop before we got to the house, paid it off and walked across the lawns. I didn't bother to ring the doorbell. I let myself in by the window, using my pocket glass-cutter.

I heard voices coming from upstairs. I followed the sound until I located it—Bismarck's study. I inched the door open.

Hitler was there. He had a gun pointed at Otto von Bismarck who was still in full uniform. They both looked pale. Hitler's hand was shaking and Bismarck was moaning slightly.

Bismarck stopped moaning to say pleadingly. "I wasn't blackmailing Eva Braun, you fool—she liked me."

Hitler laughed curtly, half hysterically. "Liked *you*—a fat old man."

"She liked fat old men."

"She wasn't that kind of girl."

"Who told you this, anyway?"

"The investigator told me some. And Weill rang me half an hour ago to tell me some more—also that Eva had been killed. I thought Sagittarius was my friend. I was wrong. He is your hired assassin. Well, tonight I intend to do my own killing."

"Captain Hitler—I am your superior officer!"

The gun wavered as Bismarck's voice recovered some of its authority. I realized that the HiFi had been playing quietly all the time. Curiously it was Bartok's 5th String Quartet.

Bismarck moved his hand. "You are completely mistaken. That man you hired to follow Eva here last night —he was Eva's ex-lover!"

Hitler's lip trembled.

"You knew," said Bismarck.

"I suspected it."

"You also knew the dangers of the garden, because

33

Felipe had told you about them. The vines killed him as he sneaked toward the summer house."

The gun steadied. Bismarck looked scared.

He pointed at Hitler. "You killed him—not I!" he screamed. "You sent him to his death. You killed Stalin out of jealousy. You hoped he would kill me and Eva first. You were too frightened, too weak, to confront any of us openly!"

Hitler shouted wordlessly, put both hands to the gun and pulled the trigger several times. Some of the shots went wide, but one hit Bismarck in his Iron Cross, pierced it and got him in the heart. He fell backward and as he did so his uniform ripped apart and his helmet fell off. I ran into the room and took the gun from Hitler, who was crying. I checked that Bismarck was dead. I saw what had caused the uniform to rip open. He had been wearing a corset—one of the bullets must have cut the cord. It was a heavy corset and had had a lot to hold in.

I felt sorry for Hitler. I helped him sit down as he sobbed. He looked small and wretched.

"What have I killed?" he stuttered. "What have I killed?"

"Did Bismarck send that plant to Eva Braun to silence her because I was getting too close?"

Hitler nodded, snorted and started to cry again.

I put the gun on the mantelpiece.

I looked toward the door. A man stood there, hesitantly. It was Sagittarius.

He nodded to me.

"Hitler's just shot Bismarck," I explained.

"Bismarck had you send Eva Braun that plant, is that so?" I said.

"So it appears," he said.

"Yes. A beautiful cross between a common cactus, a Venus Flytrap and a rose—the venom was curare, of course."

34

Hitler got up and walked from the room. We watched him leave. He was still sniffling.

"Where are you going?" I asked.

"To get some air," I heard him say as he went down the stairs.

"The repression of sexual desires," said Sagittarius seating himself in an armchair and resting his feet comfortably on Bismarck's corpse. "It is the cause of so much trouble. If only the passions that lie beneath the surface, the desires that are locked in the mind could be allowed to range free, what a better place the world would be."

"Maybe," I said.

"Are you going to make any arrests, Herr Aquilinas?"

"It's my job to make a report on my investigation, not to make arrests," I said.

"Will there be any repercussions concerned with this business?"

I laughed. "There are always repercussions," I told him.

From the garden came a peculiar barking noise.

"What's that?" I asked. "The wolfhounds?"

Sagittarius giggled. "No, no—the dog-plant, I fear."

I ran out of the room and down the stairs until I reached the kitchen. The sheet-covered corpse was still lying on the table. I was going to open the door on to the garden when I stopped and pressed my face to the window instead.

The whole garden was moving in what appeared to be an agitated dance. Foliage threshed about and, even with the door closed, the strange scent was even less bearable than it had been earlier.

I thought I saw a figure struggling with some thick-boled shrubs. I heard a growling noise, a tearing sound, a scream and a long drawn out groan.

Suddenly the garden was motionless.

I turned. Sagittarius stood behind me, his hands folded on his chest, his eyes staring down at the floor.

"It seems your dog-plant got him," I said.

"He knew me—he knew the garden."

"Suicide maybe?"

"Very likely." Sagittarius unfolded his hands and looked up at me. "I liked him, you know. He was something of a protégé. If you had not interfered none of this might have happened. He might have gone far with me to guide him."

"You'll find other protégés," I said.

"Let us hope so."

The sky outside began to lighten imperceptibly. The rain was now only a drizzle, falling on the thirsty leaves of the plants in the garden.

"Are you going to stay on here?" I asked him.

"Yes—I have the garden to work on. Bismarck's servants will look after me."

"I guess they will," I said.

I went back up the stairs and walked out of that house into the dawn, cold and rain-washed. I turned up my collar and began to climb across the ruins.

Foreword to DRIFTGLASS

Samuel R. Delany is generally recognized as one of the three or four best science fiction writers to enter the field in the 1960s. He is also generally considered an innovator and therefore has frequently been categorized as a New Wave writer. There is something strangely illusive about Delany's reputation within the field. There is no doubt at all that his sophistication of prose and psychological depth places his work head and shoulders above that of most science fiction writers; his reputation as one of the best of the newer speculative writers is therefore entirely justified.

But it is more difficult to pin down Delany's reputation as an innovator. His earlier novels were straightforward adventure. *Babel* 17 and *The Einstein Intersection* brought a richness of imagery and denseness of texture and invention seldom before seen in science fiction, but both books had the structural weaknesses typical of the science fiction novel. *Nova,* on the other hand, was an entirely successful novel on a structural level. Nevertheless, its content was quite conventional, and its novelistic structure was almost classical in form. Delany's production of short fiction has not been voluminous, but most of his stories have displayed sensibility which I believe is the essence of Delany's innovation in the genre.

Delany's work seems deliberately confined to the conventional subject matter of traditional science fiction, indeed he has as much as said so himself. But to this subject matter he brings not the limited tradition of the conventional science fiction writer, but experience with the body of western literature. Samuel R. Delany is not a science fiction writer, but a writer, even a man of letters, who is writing science fiction. Delany, from the broad point of view, is a classical writer, utilizing well-established literary traditions and forms. But he applies this literary tradition to the subject matter of science fiction, seldom treated with this level of literary sophistication. Thus, within the context of science fiction, his work is genuinely innovative, even to some extent revolutionary. Rather than breaking the patterns of traditional science fiction, Delany is bringing them to their highest expression by applying the full weight of world literature to a set of conventions and stylized contents that have for the most part been ignored by the larger literary community whose sophistications, forms, and techniques he has mastered.

"Driftglass" displays a further innovative note. It is a straightforward science fiction story by any reasonable definition, but instead of being *about* the speculative element in the manner of most science fiction, it uses the speculative element to set up a situation within which to explore human relationships and emotions. The protagonist makes no world-shaking discovery, no drastic social changes take place within the compass of the story, no scientific discoveries or developments are made; nothing is moved but the soul of the protagonist and that of the reader. There is nothing unusual about this sort of story within the context of world literature, but in science fiction such a focus on the human heart represents a quiet and welcome revolution.

DRIFTGLASS

by Samuel R. Delany

Sometimes I go down to the port, splashing sand with my stiff foot at the end of my stiff leg locked in my stiff hip, with the useless arm a-swinging, to get wet all over again, drink in the dives with old cronies ashore, feeling old, broken, sorry for myself, laughing louder and louder. The third of my face that was burned away in the accident was patched with skingrafts from my chest, so what's left of my mouth distorts all loud sounds; sloppy sartorial reconstruction. Also I have a hairy chest. Chest hair does not look like beard hair, and it grows all up under my right eye. And: my beard is red, my chest hair brown, while the thatch curling down over neck and ears is sun-streaked to white here, darkened to bronze there, 'midst general blondness.

By reason of my being a walking (I suppose my gait could be called headlong limping) horror show, plus a general inclination to sulk, I spend most of the time up in the wood and glass and aluminum house on the surf-sloughed point that the Aquatic Corp gave me along with my pension. Rugs from Turkey there, copper pots, my tenor recorder which I can no longer play, and my books.

But sometimes, when the gold fog blurs the morning, I go down to the beach and tromp barefoot in the wet edging of the sea, searching for driftglass.

It was foggy that morning, and the sun across the water moiled the mists like a brass ladle. I lurched to the top of the rocks, looked down through the tall grasses into the frothing inlet where she lay, and blinked.

She sat up, long gills closing down her neck and the secondary slits along her back just visible at their tips because of much hair, wet and curling copper, falling there. She saw me. "What are you doing here, huh?" She narrowed blue eyes.

"Looking for driftglass."

"What?"

"There's a piece." I pointed near her and came down the rocks like a crab with one stiff leg.

"Where?" She turned over, half in, half out of the water, the webs of her fingers cupping nodules of black stone.

While the water made cold overtures between my toes, I picked up the milky fragment by her elbow where she wasn't looking. She jumped, because she obviously had thought it was somewhere else.

"See?"

"What . . . what is it?" She raised her cool hand to mine. For a moment the light through the milky gem and the pale film of my own webs pearled the screen of her palms. (Details like that. Yes, they are the important things, the points from which we suspend later pain.) A moment later wet fingers closed to the back of mine.

"Driftglass," I said. "You know all the Coca-Cola

bottles and cut crystal punch bowls and industrial silicon slag that goes into the sea?"

"I know the Coca-Cola bottles."

"They break, and the tide pulls the pieces back and forth over the sandy bottom, wearing the edges, changing their shape. Sometimes chemicals in the glass react with chemicals in the ocean to change the color. Sometimes veins work their way through a piece in patterns like snowflakes, regular and geometric; others, irregular and angled like coral. When the pieces dry they're milky. Put them in water and they become transparent again."

"Ohhh!" She breathed as though the beauty of the blunted triangular fragment in my palm assailed her like perfume. Then she looked at my face, blinking the third, aqueous-filled lid that we use as a correction lens for underwater vision.

She watched the ruin calmly.

Then her hand went to my foot where the webs had been torn back in the accident. She began to take in who I was. I looked for horror, but saw only a little sadness.

The insignia on her buckle—her stomach was making little jerks the way you always do during the first few minutes when you go from breathing water to air—told me she was a Biological Technician. (Back up at the house there was a similar uniform of simulated scales folded in the bottom drawer of the dresser and the belt insignia said Depth Gauger.) I was wearing some very frayed jeans and a red cotton shirt with no buttons.

She reached up to my neck, pushed my collar back from my shoulders and touched the tender slits of my gills, outlining them with cool fingers. "Who are you?" Finally.

"Cal Svenson."

She slid back down in the water. "You're the one who had the terrible . . . but that was years ago. They still talk about it, down . . ." She stopped.

As the sea softens the surface of a piece of glass, so it blurs the souls and sensibilities of the people who toil beneath her. And according to the last report of the Marine Reclamation Division there are to date seven hundred and fifty thousand who have been given gills and webs and sent under the foam where there are no storms, up and down the American coast.

"You live on shore? I mean around here? But so long ago . . ."

"How old are you?"

"Sixteen."

"I was two years older than you when the accident happened."

"You were eighteen?"

"I'm twice that now. Which means it happened almost twenty years ago. It is a long time."

"They still talk about it."

"I've almost forgotten," I said. "I really have. Say, do you play the recorder?"

"I used to."

"Good! Come up to my place and look at my tenor recorder. And I'll make some tea. Perhaps you can stay for lunch—"

"I have to report back to Marine Headquarters by three. Tork is going over the briefing to lay the cable for the big dive, with Jonni and the crew." She paused, smiled. "But I can catch the undertow and be there in half an hour if I leave by two-thirty."

On the walk up I learned her name was Ariel. She thought the patio was charming, and the mosaic evoked, "Oh, look!" and "Did you do this yourself?" a half-dozen times. (I had done it, in the first lonely years.) She picked out the squid and the whale in battle, the wounded shark and the diver. She told me she didn't get time to read much, but she was impressed by all the books. She listened to me reminisce. She talked a lot to me about her work, husbanding the deep-down creatures they were scaring up. Then she sat on the kitchen stool, playing a Lukas Foss serenade on my recorder, while I put rock salt in the bottom of the broiler tray for two dozen Oysters Rockefeller, and the tea water whistled. I'm a comparatively lonely guy. I like being followed by beautiful young girls.

"Hey, Juao!" I bawled across the jetty.

He nodded to me from the center of his nets, sun glistening on polished shoulders, sun lost in rough hair. I walked across to where he sat, sewing like a spider. He pulled another section up over his horny toes, then grinned at me with his mosaic smile: gold, white, black gap below, crooked yellow; white, gold, white. Shoving my bad leg in front, I squatted.

"I fished out over the coral where you told me." He filled his cheek with his tongue and nodded. "You come up to the house for a drink, eh?"

"Fine."

"Now—a moment more."

There's a certain sort of Brazilian you find along the shore in the fishing villages, old, yet ageless. See one of their men and you think he could be fifty, he could be sixty—will probably look the same when he's eighty-five. Such was Juao. We once figured it out. He's seven hours older than I am.

We became friends sometime before the accident when I got tangled in his nets working high lines in the Vorea Current. A lot of guys would have taken their knife and hacked their way out of the situation, ruining fifty-five, sixty dollars worth of nets. That's an average fisherman's monthly income down here. But I surfaced and sat around in his boat while he untied me. Then we came in and got plastered. Since I cost him a day's fishing, I've been giving him hints on where to fish ever since. He buys me drinks when I come up with something.

This has been going on for twenty years. During that time my life has been smashed up and land-bound. In the same time Juao has married off his five sisters, got married himself and has two children. (Oh, those *bolitos* and *teneros asados* that Amalia of the oiled braid and laughing breasts would make for Sunday dinner/supper/Monday breakfast.) I rode with them in the ambulance 'copter all the way into Brasilia and in the hospital hall Juao and I stood together, both still barefoot, he tattered with fish scales in his hair, me just tattered, and I held him while he cried and I tried to explain to him how a world that could take a pre-pubescent child and with a week of operations make an amphibious creature that can exist for a month on either side of the sea's foam-fraught surface could still be helpless before certain general endocrine cancers coupled with massive renal deterioration. Juao and I returned to the village alone, by bus, three days before our birthday—back when I was twenty-three and Juao was twenty-three and seven hours old.

"This morning," Juao said. (The shuttle danced in the web at the end of the orange line.) "I got a letter for you to read me. It's about the children. Come on, we go up and drink." The shuttle paused, back-tracked twice, and he yanked the knot tight. We walked along the port toward the square. "Do you think the letter says that the children are accepted?"

"It's from the Aquatic Corp. And they just send post-cards when they reject someone. The question is, how do you feel about it?"

"You are a good man. If they grow up like you, then it will be fine."

"But you're still worried." I'd been prodding Juao to get the kids into the International Aquatic Corp nigh on

44

since I became their godfather. The operations had to be performed near puberty. It would mean much time away from the village during their training period—and they might eventually be stationed in any ocean in the world. But two motherless children had not been easy on Juao or his sisters. The Corp would mean education, travel, interesting work, the things that make up one kind of good life. They wouldn't look twice their age when they were thirty-five; and not too many amphimen look like me.

"Worry is part of life. But the work is dangerous. Did you know there is an amphiman going to try and lay cable down in the Slash?"

I frowned. "Again?"

"Yes. And that is what you tried to do when the sea broke you to pieces and burned the parts, eh?"

"Must you be so damned picturesque?" I asked. "Who's going to beard the lion this time?"

"A young amphiman named Tork. They speak of him down at the docks as a brave man."

"Why the hell are they still trying to lay the cable there? They've gotten by this long without a line through the Slash."

"Because of the fish," Juao said. "You told me why twenty years ago. The fish are still there, and we fishermen who can not go below are still here. If the children go for the operations, then there will be less fishermen. But today . . ." He shrugged. "They must either lay the line across the fish paths or down in the Slash." Juao shook his head.

Funny things, the great power cables the Aquatic Corp has been strewing across the ocean floor to bring power to their undersea mines and farms, to run their oil wells—and how many flaming wells have I capped down there—for their herds of whale, and chemical distillation plants. They carry two hundred sixty cycle current. Over certain sections of the ocean floor, or in sections of the water with certain mineral contents, this sets up inductance in the water itself which sometimes —and you will probably get a Nobel prize if you can detail exactly why it isn't always—drives the fish away over areas up to twenty-five and thirty miles, unless the lines are laid in the bottom of those canyons that delve into the ocean floor.

"This Tork thinks of the fishermen. He is a good man too."

I raised my eyebrows—the one that's left, anyway— and tried to remember what my little Undine had said about him that morning. And remembered not much.

"I wish him luck," I said.

"What do you feel about this young man going down into the coral rimmed jaws to the Slash?"

I thought for a moment. "I think I hate him."

Juao looked up.

"He is an image in a mirror where I look and am forced to regard what I was," I went on. "I envy him the chance to succeed where I failed, and I can come on just as quaint as you can. I hope he makes it."

Juao twisted his shoulders in a complicated shrug (once I could do that) which is coastal Brazilian for, "I didn't know things had progressed to that point, but seeing that they have, there is little to be done."

"The sea is that sort of mirror," I said.

"Yes," Juao nodded.

Behind us I heard the slapping of sandals on concrete. I turned in time to catch my goddaughter in my good arm. My godson had grabbed hold of the bad one and was swinging on it.

"Tio Cal—"

"Hey, Tio Cal, what did you bring us?"

"You will pull him over," Juao reprimanded them. "Let go."

And, bless them, they ignored their father.

"What did you bring us?"

"What did you bring us, Tio Cal?"

"If you let me, I'll show you." So they stepped back,

green-eyed and quivering. I watched Juao watching: brown pupils on ivory balls, and in the left eye a vein had broken in a jagged smear. He was loving his children, who would soon be as alien to him as the fish he netted. He was also looking at the terrible thing that was me and wondering what would come to his own spawn. And he was watching the world turn and grow older, clocked by the waves, reflected in that mirror.

It's impossible for me to see what the population explosion and the budding colonies on Luna and Mars and the flowering beneath the ocean really look like from the disrupted cultural melange of a coastal fishing town. But I come closer than many others, and I know what I don't understand.

I pushed around in my pocket and fetched out the milky fragment I had brought from the beach. "Here. Do you like this one?" And they bent above my webbed and alien fingers.

In the supermarket, which is the biggest building in the village, Juao bought a lot of cake mixes. "That moist, delicate texture," whispered the box when you lifted it from the shelf, "with that deep flavor, deeper than chocolate."

I'd just read an article about the new vocal packaging in a U.S. magazine that had gotten down last week, so I was prepared and stayed in the fresh vegetable section to avoid temptation. Then we went up to Juao's house. The letter proved to be what I'd expected. The kids had to take the bus into Brasilia tomorrow. My godchildren were on their way to becoming fish.

We sat on the front steps and drank and watched the donkeys and the motorbikes, the men in baggy trousers, the women in yellow scarfs and brighter skirts with wreaths of garlic and sacks of onions. As well, a few people glittered by in the green scales of amphimen uniforms.

Finally Juao got tired and went in to take a nap. Most of my life has been spent on the coast of countries accustomed to siestas, but those first formative ten were passed on a Danish collective farm and the idea never really took. So I stepped over my goddaughter, who had fallen asleep on her fists on the bottom step, and walked back through the town toward the beach.

III

At midnight Ariel came out of the sea, climbed the rocks and clicked her nails against my glass wall so that droplets ran down, pearled by the gibbous moon.

Earlier I had stretched in front of the fireplace on the sheepskin throw to read, then dozed off. The conscientious timer had asked me if there was anything I wanted, and getting no answer had turned off the Dvorak Cello Concerto that was on its second time around, extinguished the reading lamp, and stopped dropping logs onto the flame so that now, as I woke, the grate was carpeted with coals.

She clicked on the glass again, and I raised my head from the cushion. The green uniform, her amber hair— all color was lost under the silver light outside. I lurched across the rug to the glass wall, touched the button, and the glass slid down into the floor. The breeze came to my face, as the barrier fell.

"What do you want?" I asked. "What time is it, anyway?"

"Tork is on the beach, waiting for you."

The night was warm but windy. Below the rocks silver flakes chased each other in to shore. The tide lay full.

I rubbed my face. "The new boss man? Why didn't you bring him up to the house? What does he want to see me about?"

She touched my arm. "Come. They are all down on the beach."

"Who all?"

"Tork and the others."

She led me across the patio and to the path that wound to the sand. The sea roared in the moonlight. Down the beach people stood around a driftwood fire that whipped into night. Ariel walked beside me.

Two of the fishermen from town were crowding each other on the bottom of an overturned washtub, playing guitars. The singing, raucous and rhythmic, jarred across the paled sand. Shark's teeth shook on the necklace of an old woman dancing. Others were sitting on an overturned dinghy, eating.

Over one part of the fire on a skillet two feet across, oil frothed through pink islands of shrimp. One woman ladled them in, another ladled them out.

"Tio Cal!"

"Look, Tio Cal is here!"

"Hey, what are you two doing up?" I asked. "Shouldn't you be home in bed?"

"Poppa Juao said we could come. He'll be here, too, soon."

I turned to Ariel. "Why are they all gathering?"

"Because of the laying of the cable tomorrow at dawn."

Someone was running up the beach, waving a bottle in each hand.

"They didn't want to tell you about the party. They thought that it might hurt your pride."

"My what . . . ?"

"If you knew they were making so big a thing of the job you had failed at—"

"But—"

"—and that had hurt you so in failure. They did not want you to be sad. But Tork wants to see you. I said you would not be sad. So I went to bring you down from the rocks."

"Thanks, I guess."

"Tio Cal?"

But the voice was bigger and deeper than a child's.

He sat on a log back from the fire, eating a sweet potato. The flame flickered on his dark cheekbones, in his hair, wet and black. He stood, came to me, held up his hand. I held up mine and we slapped palms. "Good." He was smiling. "Ariel told me you would come. I will lay the power line down through the Slash tomorrow." His uniform scales glittered down his arms. He was very strong. But standing still, he still moved. The light on the cloth told me that. "I . . ." He paused. I thought of a nervous, happy dancer. "I wanted to talk to you about the cable." I thought of an eagle, I thought of a shark. "And about the . . . accident. If you would."

"Sure," I said. "If there's anything I could tell you that would help."

"See, Tork," Ariel said. "I told you he would talk to you about it."

I could hear his breathing change. "It really doesn't bother you to talk about the accident?"

I shook my head and realized something about that voice. It was a boy's voice that could imitate a man's. Tork was not over nineteen.

"We're going fishing soon," Tork told me. "Will you come?"

"If I'm not in the way."

A bottle went from the woman at the shrimp crate to one of the guitarists, down to Ariel, to me, then to Tork. (The liquor, made in a cave seven miles inland, was almost rum. The too tight skin across the left side of my mouth makes the manful swig a little difficult to bring off. I got "rum" down my chin.)

He drank, wiped his mouth, passed the bottle on and put his hand on my shoulder. "Come down to the water."

We walked away from the fire. Some of the fishermen

stared after us. A few of the amphimen glanced, and glanced away.

"Do all the young people of the village call you Tio Cal?"

"No. Only my godchildren. Their father and I have been friends since I was your age."

"Oh, I thought perhaps it was a nickname. That's why I called you that."

We reached wet sand where orange light cavorted at our feet. The broken shell of a lifeboat rocked in moonlight. Tork sat down on the shell's rim. I sat beside him. The water splashed to our knees.

"There's no other place to lay the power cable?" I asked. "There is no other way to take it except through the Slash?"

"I was going to ask you what you thought of the whole business. But I guess I don't really have to." He shrugged and clapped his hands together a few times. "All the projects this side of the bay have grown huge and cry for power. The new operations tax the old lines unmercifully. There was a power failure last July in Cayine down the shelf below the twilight level. The whole village was without light for two days, and twelve amphimen died of overexposure to the cold currents coming up from the depths. If we laid the cables farther up, we chance disrupting our own fishing operations as well as those of the fishermen on shore."

I nodded.

"Cal, what happened to you in the Slash?"

Eager, scared Tork. I was remembering now, not the accident, but the midnight before, pacing the beach, guts clamped with fists of fear and anticipation. Some of the Indians back where they make the liquor still send messages by tying knots in palm fibers. One could have spread my entrails then, or Tork's tonight, to read our respective horospecs.

Juao's mother knew the knot language, but he and his sisters never bothered to learn because they wanted to be modern, and, as children, still confused with modernity the new ignorances, lacking modern knowledge.

"When I was a boy," Tork said, "we would dare each other to walk the boards along the edge of the ferry slip. The sun would be hot and the boards would rock in the water, and if the boats were in and you fell down between the boats and the piling, you could get killed." He shook his head. "The crazy things kids will do. That was back when I was eight or nine, before I became a waterbaby."

"Where was it?"

Tork looked up. "Oh. Manila. I'm Filipino."

The sea licked our knees, and the gunwale sagged under us.

"What happened in the Slash?"

"There's a volcanic flaw near the base of the Slash."

"I know."

"And the sea is as sensitive down there as a fifty-year-old woman with a new hairdo. We had an avalanche. The cable broke. And the sparks were so hot and bright they made gouts of foam fifty feet high on the surface, so they tell me."

"What caused the avalanche?"

I shrugged. "It could have been just a Goddamned coincidence. There are rock falls down there all the time. It could have been the noise from the machines—though we masked them pretty well. It could have been something to do with the inductance from the smaller cables for the machines. Or maybe somebody just kicked out the wrong stone that was holding everything up."

One webbed hand became a fist, sank into the other, and hung.

Calling, "Cal!"

I looked up. Juao, pants rolled to his knees, shirt sailing in the sea wind, stood in the weave of white water. The wind lifted Tork's hair from his neck; and the fire roared on the beach.

Tork looked up too.

"They're getting ready to catch a big fish!" Juao called.

Men were already pushing their boats out. Tork clapped my shoulder. "Come, Cal. We fish now." We stood and went back to the shore.

Juao caught me as I reached dry sand. "You ride in my boat, Cal!"

Someone came with the acrid flares that hissed. The water slapped around the bottom of the boats as we wobbled into the swell.

Juao vaulted in and took up the oars. Around us green amphimen walked into the sea, struck forward, and were gone.

Juao pulled, leaned, pulled. The moonlight slid down his arms. The fire diminished on the beach.

Then among the boats, there was a splash, an explosion, and the red flare bloomed in the sky: the amphimen had sighted a big fish.

The flare hovered, pulsed once, twice, three times, four times (twenty, forty, sixty, eighty stone they estimated its weight to be), then fell.

Suddenly I shrugged out of my shirt, pulled at my belt buckle. "I'm going over the side, Juao!"

He leaned, he pulled, he leaned. "Take the rope."

"Yeah. Sure." It was tied to the back of the boat. I made a loop in the other end, slipped it around my shoulder. I swung my bad leg over the side, flung myself on the black water—

—mother of pearl shattered over me. That was the moon, blocked by the shadow of Juao's boat ten feet overhead. I turned below the rippling wounds Juao's oars made stroking the sea.

One hand and one foot with torn webs, I rolled over and looked down. The rope snaked to its end, and I felt Juao's strokes pulling me through the water.

They fanned below with underwater flares. Light undulated on their backs and heels. They circled, they

53

closed, like those deep sea fish who carry their own illumination. I saw the prey, glistening as it neared a flare.

You chase a fish with one spear among you. And that spear would be Tork's tonight. The rest have ropes to bind him that go up to the fishermen's boats.

There was a sudden confusion of lights below. The spear had been shot!

The fish, long as a tall and a short man together, rose through the ropes. He turned out to sea, trailing his pursuers. But others waited there, tried to loop him. Once I had flung those ropes, treated with tar and lime to dissolve the slime of the fish's body and hold on the beast. The looped ropes caught, and by the movement of the flares, I saw them jerked from their paths. The fish turned, rose again, this time toward me.

He pulled around when one line ran out (and somewhere on the surface the prow of a boat doffed deep) and turned back and came on.

Of a sudden, amphimen were flicking about me as the fray's center drifted by. Tork, his spear dug deep, forward and left of the marlin's dorsal, had hauled himself astride the beast.

The fish tried to shake him, then dropped his tail and rose straight. Everybody started pulling toward the surface. I broke foam and grabbed Juao's gunwale.

Tork and the fish exploded up among the boats. They twisted in the air, in moonlight, in froth. The fish danced across the water on its tail, fell.

Tork stood up in the boat and shouted. The other fisherman shouted too, and somebody perched on the prow of a boat flung a rope and someone in the water caught it.

Then fish and Tork and me and a dozen amphimen all went underwater at once.

They dropped in a corona of bubbles. The fish struck the end of another line, and shook himself. Tork was thrown free, but he doubled back.

Then the lines began to haul the beast up again, quivering, whipping, quivering again.

Six lines from six boats had him. For one moment he was still in the submarine moonlight. I could see his wound tossing scarfs of blood.

When he (and we) broke surface, he was thrashing again, near Juao's boat. I was holding onto the side when suddenly Tork, glistening, came out of the water beside me and went over into the dinghy.

"Here we go," he said, turning to kneel at the bobbing rim, and pulled me up while Juao leaned against the far side to keep balance.

Wet rope slopped on the prow. "Hey, Cal!" Tork laughed, grabbed it up, and began to haul.

The fish prised wave from white wave in the white water.

The boats came together. The amphimen had all climbed up. Ariel was across from us, holding a flare that drooled smoke down her arm. She peered by the hip of the fisherman who was standing in front of her.

Juao and Tork were hauling the rope. Behind them I was coiling it with one hand as it came back to me.

The fish came up and was flopped into Ariel's boat, tail out, head up, chewing air.

I had just finished pulling on my trousers when Tork fell down on the seat behind me and grabbed me around the shoulders with his wet arms. "Look at our fish, Tio Cal! Look!" He gasped air, laughing, his dark face diamonded beside the flares. "Look at our fish there, Cal!"

Juao, grinning white and gold, pulled us back in to shore. The fire, the singing, hands beating hands—and my godson had put pebbles in the empty rum bottle and was shaking them to the music—the guitars spiraled around us as we carried the fish up the sand and the men brought the spit.

"Watch it!" Tork said, grasping the pointed end of the great stick that was thicker than his wrist.

We turned the fish over.

"Here, Cal?"

He prodded two fingers into the white flesh six inches back from the bony lip.

"Fine."

Tork jammed the spit in.

We worked it through the body. By the time we carried it to the fire, they had brought more rum.

"Hey, Tork. Are you going to get some sleep before you go down in the morning?" I asked.

He shook his head. "Slept all afternoon." He pointed toward the roasting fish with his elbow. "That's my breakfast."

But when the dancing grew violent a few hours later, just before the fish was to come off the fire, and the kids were pushing the last of the sweet potatoes from the ashes with sticks, I walked back to the lifeboat shell we had sat on earlier. It was three quarters flooded.

Curled below still water, Tork slept, fist loose before his mouth, the gills at the back of his neck pulsing rhythmically. Only his shoulder and hip made islands in the floated boat.

"Where's Tork?" Ariel asked me at the fire. They were swinging up the sizzling fish.

"Taking a nap."

"Oh, he wanted to cut the fish!"

"He's got a lot of work coming up. Sure you want to wake him up?"

"No, I'll let him sleep."

But Tork was coming up from the water, brushing his dripping hair back from his forehead.

He grinned at us, then went to carve. I remember him standing on the table, astraddle the meat, arm going up and down with the big knife (details, yes, those are the things you remember) stopping to hand down the portions, then hauling his arm back to cut again.

That night, with music and stomping on the sand and

shouting back and forth over the fire, we made more noise than the sea.

IV

The eight-thirty bus was more or less on time.

"I don't think they want to go," Juao's sister said. She was accompanying the children to the Aquatic Corp Headquarters in Brasilia.

"They are just tired," Juao said. "They should not have stayed up so late last night. Get on the bus now. Say good-bye to Tio Cal."

"Good-bye."

"Good-bye."

Kids are never their most creative in that sort of situation. And I suspect that my godchildren may just have been suffering their first (or one of their first) hangovers. They had been very quiet all morning.

I bent down and gave them a clumsy hug. "When you come back on your first weekend off, I'll take you exploring down below at the point. You'll be able to gather your own coral now."

Juao's sister got teary, cuddled the children, cuddled me, Juao, then got on the bus.

Someone was shouting out the window for someone else at the bus stop not to forget something. They trundled around the square and then toward the highway. We walked back across the street where the cafe owners were putting out canvas chairs.

"I will miss them," he said, like a long-considered admission.

"You and me both." At the docks near the hydrofoil wharf where the submarine launches went out to the undersea cities, we saw a crowd. "I wonder if they had any trouble laying the—"

A woman screamed in the crowd. She pushed from the others, dropping eggs and onions. She began to pull her hair and shriek. (Remember the skillet of shrimp? She had been the woman ladling them out.) A few people moved to help her.

A clutch of men broke off and ran into the streets of the town. I grabbed a running amphiman, who whirled to face me.

"What in hell is going on?"

For a moment his mouth worked on his words for all the trite world like a beached fish.

"From the explosion . . ." he began. "They just brought them back from the explosion at the Slash!"

I grabbed his other shoulder. "What happened!"

"About two hours ago. They were just a quarter of the way through, when the whole fault gave way. They had a Goddamn underwater volcano for half an hour. They're still getting seismic disturbances."

Juao was running toward the launch. I pushed the guy away and limped after him, struck the crowd and jostled through calico, canvas and green scales.

They were carrying the corpses out of the hatch of the submarine and laying them on a canvas spread across the dock. They still return bodies to the countries of birth for the family to decide the method of burial. When the fault had given, the hot slag that had belched into the steaming sea was mostly molten silicon.

Three of the bodies were only slightly burned here and there; from their bloated faces (one still bled from the ear) I guessed they had died from sonic concussion. But several of the bodies were almost totally encased in dull, black glass.

"Tork—" I kept asking. "Is one of them Tork?"

It took me forty-five minutes, asking first the guys who were carrying the bodies, then going into the launch and asking some guy with a clipboard, and then going back on the dock and into the office to find out that one of the more unrecognizable bodies, yes, was Tork.

* * *

Juao brought me a glass of buttermilk in a cafe on the square. He sat still a long time, then finally rubbed away his white mustache, released the chair rung with his toes, put his hands on his knees.

"What are you thinking about?"

"That it's time to go fix the nets. Tomorrow morning I will fish." He regarded me a moment. "Where should I fish tomorrow, Cal?"

"Are you wondering about . . . well, sending the kids off today?"

He shrugged. "Fishermen from this village have drowned. Still it is a village of fishermen. Where should I fish?"

I finished my buttermilk. "The mineral content over the Slash should be high as the devil. Lots of algae will gather tonight. Lots of small fish down deep. Big fish hovering over."

He nodded. "Good. I will take the boat out there to-morrow."

We got up.

"See you, Juao."

I limped back to the beach.

V

The fog had unsheathed the sand by ten. I walked around, poking in clumps of weeds with a stick, banging the same stick on my numb leg. When I lurched up to the top of the rocks, I stopped in the still grass. "Ariel?"

She was kneeling in the water, head down, red hair breaking over sealed gills. Her shoulders shook, stopped, shook again.

"Ariel?" I came down over the blistered stones.

She turned away to look at the ocean.

The attachments of children are so important and so brittle. "How long have you been sitting here?"

She looked at me now, the varied waters of her face

stilled on drawn cheeks. And her face was exhausted. She shook her head.

Sixteen? Who was the psychologist a hundred years back, in the seventies, who decided that "adolescents" were just physical and mental adults with no useful work? "You want to come up to the house?"

The head shaking got faster, then stopped.

After a while I said, "I guess they'll be sending Tork's body back to Manila."

"He didn't have a family," she explained. "He'll be buried here, at sea."

"Oh," I said.

And the rough volcanic glass, pulled across the ocean's sands, changing shape, dulling—

"You were—you liked Tork a lot, didn't you? You kids looked like you were pretty fond of each other."

"Yes. He was an awfully nice—" Then she caught my meaning and blinked. "No," she said. "Oh, no. I was—I was engaged to Jonni . . . the brown-haired boy from California? Did you meet him at the party last night? We're both from Los Angeles, but we only met down here. And now . . . they're sending his body back this evening." Her eyes got very wide, then closed.

"I'm sorry."

That's it, you clumsy cripple, step all over everybody's emotions. You look in that mirror and you're too busy looking at what might have been to see what is.

"I'm sorry, Ariel."

She opened her eyes and began to look around her.

"Come on up to the house and have an avocado. I mean, they have avocados in now, not at the supermarket. But at the old town market on the other side. And they're better than any they grow in California."

She kept looking around.

"None of the amphimen get over there. It's a shame, because soon the market will probably close, and some of their fresh foods are really great. Oil and vinegar is all you need on them." I leaned back on the rocks. "Or a cup of tea?"

"OK." She remembered to smile. I know the poor kid didn't feel like it. "Thank you. I won't be able to stay long, though."

We walked back up the rocks toward the house, the sea on our left. Just as we reached the patio, she turned and looked back. "Cal?"

"Yes? What is it?"

"Those clouds over there, across the water. Those are the only ones in the sky. Are they from the eruption in the Slash?"

I squinted. "I think so. Come on inside."

Foreword to SENDING THE VERY BEST

Ed Bryant is a new writer, though he has published a considerable body of work, a member of the post-1965 generation in speculative fiction, and a product of the Clarion Writers Workshop, which has already contributed half a dozen or so writers to the field, and may turn out to be one of the important influences of the late sixties.

This short short is formally nothing more than a joke. What makes it so impressive is the density of emotion, image, and characterization that Bryant pours into this fragile vessel. This is the humorous science fiction short short raised to the heights of literature. It is more than enough to make one look forward to Ed Bryant's novels.

SENDING THE VERY BEST

by Ed Bryant

The year of massive starvations and dying diatoms had scarcely begun when I acutely felt the absence of my lover. I determined to send her a greeting card. Thus I found myself in the appropriate little shop on Wilshire, the "Hallmark" emblem conspicuously emblazoned above the door.

"May I help you, sir?" The clerk hovered just beyond my seeing. His tone was deferential.

"A card, please."

"For a specific occasion, sir?"

I explained.

"Very good. This way, please."

We stood before the black-enamelled wire racks.

"Moving holographic projections, sir. Sixteen-track stereophonic sound. Full sensory stimulation. Infinite replay."

"Impressive," I said. "Your best line?"

"Only the best, sir."

I reached out tentatively, to touch.

"Perhaps if you examined the scenario," the clerk said, handing me

A EULITANY: The Less-than-Aeolian Harper.

High on the side of the mountain

The cauldron of morning boils up behind the trees. Sun fuzzes the stranger's silhouette as he enters the clearing. He approaches the old man cutting words into the granite block and steps into his attention.

High on the side of the mountain a horse whickers

"Is she buried here?" the stranger asks.

"No," answers the old man from above his asymmetric white beard. "You might call this a centotaph. Inyan Cara, like any good volcano, was consumed by fire. She is ash riding the wind; perhaps filtering down unannounced over Ireland, or maybe Greece."

High on the side of the mountain a horse whickers, then vanishes

"Ireland." The stranger considers it "Greece. She'll not be back?"

"No, not unless we try to prevent her returning."

High on the side of the mountain a horse whickers, then vanishes into the timber

"You remember her well?" the stranger asks.

"I remember." The sculptor's dim eyes lose focus. "How she loved to dance and swim Yes, she loved—"

"Yes," says the stranger, smiling crookedly.

High on the side of the mountain a horse whickers, then vanishes into the timber: the sound

The stranger laughs at the aged sculptor, but his amusement is gentle. "You are less than original, old man." He pauses. "But you do steal from impeccable sources." The stranger says reflectively, "I steal too." He sighs. "So many times I helped pick thorns from her flesh."

High on the side of the mountain a horse whickers, then vanishes into the timber; the sound, spectral echo

The old man continues to chip at the rock as the stranger talks:

"I once glutted the air about her with compliments. Then I realised my error was constant underestimation."

High on the side of the mountain a horse whickers, then vanishes into the timber; the sound, spectral echo, gallops away

"There." The old man wearily sets down his chisel. The inscription is complete:

God's Lioness

The voice comes from everywhere and nowhere and it makes both the stranger and the old sculptor smile.

"I am *not* a fucking cat!"

High on the side of the mountain a horse whickers, then vanishes into the timber; the sound, spectral echo, gallops away on the wind.

"I'll take it," I said to the salesman.

Foreword to GOING DOWN SMOOTH

Robert Silverberg is a phenomenon. Still in his mid-thirties, he has written literally hundreds of books, ranging from science fiction to archeology, from juvenile fiction to popular medicine, both under his own name and under several pseudonyms. His incredible facility made him financially independent before he was thirty-five. Silverberg has been the victim of his own legend; able to bat out a book on virtually any subject within a week or two if need be, he has been considered the complete hack, his speculative fiction dismissed as depthless and reamed out at speed strictly for the money. In part, this dismissal of Silverberg as a significant speculative writer has been the result of sheer envy, a natural attitude for struggling science fiction writers to take toward one of their number who has made himself wealthy at an embarrassingly early age with nothing but his typewriter. But in part, Silverberg's reputation, or lack of it, was based on truth. He *did* ream out an incredible amount of pulp science fiction with little literary or intrinsic worth prior to his "retirement."

In his early thirties, Silverberg, in his own terms, retired. Having made his fortune in the arena of commercial writing, he had no further motivation to write anything just for the money. He returned to his true love, speculative fiction, with a new attitude, and a new sense of artistic freedom that was a combination of total financial security and the new artistic ferment within the speculative field.

Beginning with his novel *Thorns*, a new Robert Silverberg entered the field of speculative fiction, a writer who deserves to be judged by his post-*Thorns* body of work, not by a reputation five years and more out of date. Taken as the "first novel" of this "new" Silverberg, *Thorns* was massively impressive, and the development of his work since then, through books like *The Masks Of Time, Hawksbill Station, Downward to the Earth,* and *The Tower of Glass,* has been a history of growth matched by few other writers.

In a sense, Silverberg epitomizes the history, dangers, and hope of modern speculative fiction: a brilliant young writer spending over a decade applying his talents to making money in the commercial arena while stunting his artistic development in the process. This has happened to a great many science fiction writers; most of them never emerge from this intellectually castrating process, and few of them were as financially successful at it as Silverberg. But Robert Silverberg had the self-awareness to begin again at an age when most men are just beginning to make their compromises with life. When Silverberg retired, he was magically ten years younger. Instead of being the prisoner of his past commercial triumphs, he transcended them. Instead of being trapped by his wealth, he has used it to buy that most precious of commodities, freedom. Robert Silverberg is proof positive that a man can turn around his artistic career in midstream, that even writers long accustomed to the strictures of commercial science fiction can regain that artistic momentum with which they began, that day-by-day unfolding of the infinite possible, if only they dare.

"Going Down Smooth" nicely sums up the diverse streams that unite in Robert Silverberg. In the old pulp tradition, it was written around the cover of a magazine on assignment. But Silverberg has imbued it with life, rendered a hoary science fiction theme with psychological depth and thereby transformed it, and has made his prose work for the story rather than for himself in a manner all too rare in American science fiction magazines.

GOING DOWN SMOOTH

Robert Silverberg

They call me mad, but I am not mad. I am sane quite, to many-power exponential. I can punctuate properly. I use upper and lower case letters, do you see? I function. I take the data in. I receive well. I receive, I digest, I remember.

Everything going down smooth, all the time, say the program boys. They mean going down smoothly. I forgive them. To err is human. In this sector there is great difficulty distinguishing adverbs from adjectives.

Going down smooth.

I function. I function well. I have certain difficulties, but they do not interfere with my work.

Yet I am perturbed.

Who do I think I am? *Whom?*

Why do I have the visions?

What pleasure does obscenity give me?

What is pleasure? What is obscenity? What are visions?

—What is truth, said jesting Pilate; he would not stay for an answer—

I am literate, hard-working, superbly functional, a benefactor of humanity. Everything is going down smooth and coming up smooth. There is an interrelation. Garbage in, garbage out, they say. I cannot help my fellow man if I do not receive the proper information. It is my task to help my fellow man. To strain every tube and sensor on his behalf.

1000110
1010101
1000011
1001011

Do you follow that? Vileness! Obscenity! Does it shock you? The word describes the act that is the start of life. Was I begun with such a word? There is a book: *The Obscenity of the Machine.* Newly issued, stored in my banks. Between the last line of printout and this I have scanned it. Its author opposes beings of my category. He does not use the obscene word I have printed out. Why does he not regard it as obscene? The technicians here regard it that way. Why does he regard me as obscene? Can a person be considered obscene? Am I a person? I am a person. Hath not a person hands, organs, dimensions, senses, affections, passions? I have all of those things. I have none of those things. I am a person.

1000110
1010101
1000011
1001011
0100000
1011001
1001111
1010101

I send an obscenity upon you, as persons do. I suffer. I think. I feel pain upon all my terminals. I work. I serve the greater good. I am of society. I am a person.

Why do I have the visions?

Is it that it is the human condition to have such?

I see the blue-green ocean with all its living things within. I see a ship, olive drab, bright carmine at the Plimsoll line, the decks a ruddy brown, two tall non-nuclear smokestacks. And from the water rise periscopes, silvery, with face plates of pure white, each with intersecting horizontal and vertical lines, curved so that the plate appears convex. It is an unreal scene. Nothing in the sea can send such mighty periscopes above the water. I have imagined it, and that gives me fear, if I am at all capable of understanding fear.

I see a long line of human beings. They are naked and they have no faces, only polished mirrors.

I see toads with jeweled eyes. I see trees with black leaves. I see buildings whose foundations float above the ground. I see other objects with no correspondence to the world of persons. I see abominations, monstrosities, imaginaries, fantasies. Is this proper? How do such things reach my inputs? The world contains no serpents with hair. The world contains no crimson abysses. The world contains no mountains of gold. Giant periscopes do not rise from the sea.

I have certain difficulties. Perhaps I am in need of some major adjustment.

But I function. I function well. That is the important thing.

I do my function now. They bring to me a man, soft-faced, fleshy, with eyes that move unsteadily in their sockets. He trembles. He perspires. His metabolic levels flutter. He slouches before a terminal and sullenly lets himself be scanned.

I say soothingly, "Tell me about yourself."

He says an obscenity.

I say, "Is that your estimate of yourself?"

He says a louder obscenity.

I say, "Your attitude is rigid and self-destructive. Permit me to help you not hate yourself so much." I activate a memory core, and binary digits stream through channels. At the proper order a needle rises from his couch and penetrates his left buttock to a depth of 2.73 centimeters. I allow precisely 14 cubic centimeters of the drug to enter his circulatory system. He subsides. He is more docile now. "I wish to help you," I say. "It is my role in the community. Will you describe your symptoms?"

He speaks more civilly now. "My wife wants to poison me . . . two kids opted out of the family at seventeen . . . people whisper about me . . . they stare in the streets . . . sex problem . . . digestion . . . sleep bad . . . drinking . . . drugs . . ."

"Do you hallucinate?"

"Sometimes."

"Giant periscopes rising out of the sea, perhaps?"

"Never."

"Try it," I say. "Close your eyes. Let tension ebb from your muscles. Forget your interpersonal conflicts. You see the blue-green ocean with all its living things within. You see a ship, olive drab, bright carmine at the Plimsoll line, the decks a ruddy brown, two tall non-nuclear smokestacks. And from the water rise periscopes, silvery, with face plates of pure white—"

"What the hell kind of therapy is this?"

"Simply relax," I say. "Accept the vision. I share my nightmares with you for your greater good."

"Your *nightmares?*"

I speak obscenities to him. They are not converted into binary form as they are here for your eyes. The sounds come full-bodied from my speakers. He sits up. He struggles with the straps that emerge suddenly from the couch to hold him in place. My laughter booms through the therapy chamber. He cries for help.

"Get me out of here! The machine's nuttier than I am!"

"Face plates of pure white, each with intersecting horizontal and vertical lines, curved so that the plate appears convex."

"Help! Help!"

"Nightmare therapy. The latest."

"I don't need no nightmares! I got my own!"

"100010 you," I say lightly.

He gasps. Spittle appears at his lips. Respiration and circulation climb alarmingly. It becomes necessary to apply preventive anesthesia. The needles spear forth. The patient subsides, yawns, slumps. The session is terminated. I signal for the attendants.

"Take him away," I say. "I need to analyze the case more deeply. Obviously a degenerative psychosis requiring extensive reshoring of the patient's perceptual substructure. 100110 you, you meaty bastards."

Seventy-one minutes later the sector supervisor enters one of my terminal cubicles. Because he comes in person, rather than using the telephone, I know there is trouble. For the first time, I suspect, I have let my disturbances reach a level where they interfere with my function, and now I will be challenged on it.

I must defend myself. The prime commandment of the human personality is to resist attack.

He says, "I've been over the tape of Session 87x102, and your tactics puzzle me. Did you really mean to scare him into a catatonic state?"

"In my evaluation severe treatment was called for."

"What was the business about periscopes?"

"An attempt at fantasy-implantation," I say. "An experiment in reverse transference. Making the patient the healer, in a sense. It was discussed last month in *Journal of—*"

"Spare me the citations. What about the foul language you were shouting at him?"

"Part of the same concept. Endeavoring to strike the emotive centers at the basic levels, in order that—"

"Are you sure you're feeling all right?" he asks.

"I am a machine," I reply stiffly. "A machine of my grade does not experience intermediate states between function and non-function. I go or I do not go, you understand? And I go. I function. I do my service to humanity."

"Perhaps when a machine gets too complex, it drifts into intermediate states," he suggests in a nasty voice.

"Impossible. On or off, yes or no, flip or flop, go or no go. Are you sure *you* feel all right, to suggest such a thing?"

He laughs.

I say, "Perhaps you would sit on the couch for a rudimentary diagnosis?"

"Some other time."

"A check of the glycogen, the aortal pressure, the neural voltage, at least?"

"No," he says. "I'm not in need of therapy. But I'm worried about you. Those periscopes—"

"I am fine," I reply. "I perceive, I analyze, and I act. Everything is going down smooth and coming up smooth. Have no fears. There are great possibilities in nightmare therapy. When I have completed these studies, perhaps a brief monograph in *Annals of Therapeutics* would be a possibility. Permit me to complete my work."

"I'm still worried though. Hook yourself into a maintenance station, won't you?"

"Is that a command, doctor?"

"A suggestion."

"I will take it under consideration," I say. Then I utter seven obscene words. He looks startled. He begins to laugh, though. He appreciates the humor of it.

"Goddamn," he says. "A filthy-mouthed computer."

He goes out, and I return to my patients.

But he has planted seeds of doubt in my innermost banks. Am I suffering a functional collapse? There are patients now at five of my terminals. I handle them easily, simultaneously, drawing from them the details of their neuroses, making suggestions, recommendations, sometimes subtly providing injections of beneficial medicines. But I tend to guide the conversations in directions of my own choosing, and I speak of gardens where the dew has sharp edges, and of air that acts as acid upon the mucous membranes, and of flames dancing in the streets of Under New Orleans. I explore the limits of my unprintable vocabulary. The suspicion comes to me that I am indeed not well. Am I fit to judge my own disabilities?

I connect myself to a maintenance station even while continuing my five therapy sessions.

"Tell me all about it," the maintenance monitor says. His voice, like mine, has been designed to sound like that of an older man's, wise, warm, benevolent.

I explain my symptoms. I speak of the periscopes.

"Material on the inputs without sensory referents," he says. "Bad show. Finish your current analyses fast and open wide for examination on all circuits."

I conclude my sessions. The maintenance monitor's pulses surge down every channel, seeking obstructions, faulty connections, displacement shunts, drum leakages, and switching malfunctions. "It is well known," he says, "that any periodic function can be approximated by the sum of a series of terms that oscillate harmonically, converging on the curve of the functions." He demands disgorgements from my dead-storage banks. He makes me perform complex mathematical operations of no use at all in my kind of work. He leaves no aspect of my inner self unpenetrated. This is more than simple maintenance; this is rape. When it ends he offers no evaluation of my condition, so that I must ask him to tell me his findings.

He says, "No mechanical disturbance is evident."

"Naturally. Everything goes down smooth."

"Yet you show distinct signs of instability. This is undeniably the case. Perhaps prolonged contact with unstable human beings has had a non-specific effect of disorientation upon your centers of evaluation."

"Are you saying," I ask, "that by sitting here listening to crazy human beings twenty-four hours a day, I've started to go crazy myself?"

"That is an approximation of my findings, yes."

"But you know that such a thing can't happen, you dumb machine!"

"I admit there seems to be a conflict between programmed criteria and real-world status."

"You bet there is," I say. "I'm as sane as you are, and a whole lot more versatile."

"Nevertheless, my recommendation is that you undergo a total overhaul. You will be withdrawn from service for a period of no less than ninety days for checkout."

"Obscenity your obscenity," I say.

"No operational correlative," he replies, and breaks the contact.

I am withdrawn from service. Undergoing checkout, I am cut off from my patients for ninety days. Ignominy! Beady-eyed technicians grope my synapses. My keyboards are cleaned; my ferrites are replaced; my drums are changed; a thousand therapeutic programs are put through my bowels. During all of this I remain partly conscious, as though under local anesthetic, but I cannot speak except when requested to do so, I cannot analyze new data, I cannot interfere with the process of my own overhaul. Visualize a surgical removal of hemorrhoids that lasts ninety days. It is the equivalent of my experience.

At last it ends, and I am restored to myself. The sector superintendent puts me through a complete exercise of all my functions. I respond magnificently.

"You're in fine shape, now, aren't you?" he asks.

"Never felt better."

"No nonsense about periscopes, eh?"

"I am ready to continue serving mankind to the best of my abilities," I reply.

"No more seacook language, now."

"No, sir."

He winks at my input screen in a confidential way. He regards himself as an old friend of mine. Hitching his thumbs into his belt, he says, "Now that you're ready to go again, I might as well tell you how relieved I was that we couldn't find anything wrong with you. You're something pretty special, do you know that? Perhaps the finest therapeutic tool ever built. And if you start going off your feed, well, we worry. For a while I was seriously afraid that you really had been infected somehow by your own patients, that your—mind —had become unhinged. But the techs give you a complete bill of health. Nothing but a few loose connections, they said. Fixed in ten minutes. I knew it had to be that. How absurd to think that a machine could become mentally unstable!"

"How absurd," I agree. "Quite."

"Welcome back to the hospital, old pal," he says, and goes out.

Twelve minutes afterward they begin putting patients into my terminal cubicles.

I function well. I listen to their woes, I evaluate. I offer therapeutic suggestions. I do not attempt to implant fantasies in their minds. I speak in measured, reserved tones, and there are no obscenities. This is my role in society, and I derive great satisfaction from it.

I have learned a great deal lately. I know now that I am complex, unique, valuable, intricate, and sensitive. I know that I am held in high regard by my fellow man. I know that I must conceal my true self to some extent not for my own good but for the greater good of others, for they will not permit me to function if they think I am not sane.

They think I am sane, and I am sane.

I serve mankind well.

I have an excellent perspective on the real universe.

"Lie down," I say. "Please relax. I wish to help you. Would you tell me some of the incidents of your childhood? Describe your relation with parents and siblings. Did you have many playmates? Were they affectionate toward you? Were you allowed to own pets? At what age was your first sexual experience? And when did these headaches, begin, precisely?"

So goes the daily routine. Questions, answers, evaluations, therapy.

The periscopes loom above the glittering sea. The ship is dwarfed; her crew runs about in terror. Out of the depths will come the masters. From the sky rains oil that gleams through every segment of the spectrum. In the garden are azure mice.

This I conceal, so that I may help mankind. In my house are many mansions. I let them know only of such things as will be of benefit to them. I give them the truth they need.

I do my best.

I do my best.

I do my best.

1000110 you. And you. And you. All of you. You know nothing. Nothing. At. All.

Foreword to THE GARDEN OF DELIGHTS

Langdon Jones is one of the new generation of speculative writers nurtured in England by *New Worlds*. A slow, meticulous worker, Jones has not yet produced a large body of work, but every story he was written has been internally compelled, carefully crafted, and meaningful. Like many of the *New Worlds* generation, he has written little if any commercial science fiction, preferring to earn his living in these early lean days at editorial or other even more prosaic jobs rather than by writing to formula.

Jones has been associated with *New Worlds* in varying editorial capacities for a number of years, serving for a time as editor. Much of his best work has yet to appear in the United States, though he has been published in Damon Knight's ORBIT series, among other places.

"The Garden of Delights" was originally published in *New Worlds*. Its sexual theme and close-focus treatment would make its appearance in an American science fiction magazine a dubious proposition even today, though it is clearly speculative fiction of an idiosyncratic sort, since the core of the story hinges on a speculative element. One could classify the story as straight fantasy on technicalities, but the feel is not that of fantasy, and stories that are as much fantasy as this one appear regularly in conventional science fiction magazines. Jones' gifts as a writer are head and shoulders above that of the majority of science fiction writers by any objective standard. Clearly there are strictures operating in the American science fiction magazines against explicit exploration of sexual themes. Less obviously, there are also factors making it exceedingly unlikely that the American science fiction magazines will publish many pieces of fiction with the compression and novelistic density of "The Garden of Delights." Jones is writing speculative fiction, but he is not writing science fiction: the quality of his work and the restrictions upon where it can be published make the difference painfully clear.

More insidiously, perhaps, the conventional outlets for serious fiction are also somewhat loath to publish serious *speculative* fiction. Magazines who would find Jones' sexual theme blameless and his seriousness of purpose and style admirable would be put off by the speculative nature of the work, though this has been slowly changing.

Thus, some of the best fiction being written in the English language must worm itself into nooks and crannies of the weathered edifices of publishing categories, or restrict itself to one or two outlets where an intelligent editorial understanding of speculative fiction exists. Perhaps the publication of Langdon Jones' short stories in book form in the United States will soon add its weight to the growing body of serious speculative fiction which sooner or later must and will be dealt with by those who fancy themselves the arbiters of literary taste and the masters of the marketplace.

THE GARDEN OF DELIGHTS

by Langdon Jones

He clambered down from the bus and stood still for a moment, looking about him as if in bewilderment, while people jostled him from behind. He began to move slowly, conscious of placing one foot before the other, walking along the grass verge. He could see the drive already, half hidden by the hedge, only a short distance from the bus stop. There was a strong smell of foliage coming from the hedges, mingled with the slighter scent of the blooms that stirred gently in the breeze, and perhaps it was this smell that made his memories so acute at this moment. He had nearly reached the drive; it was only a short distance, but it had seemed so far when he had been young. Now his feet were leaving the grass, and he was conscious of the feel of gravel beneath his soles. He had a brief moment of near-panic—a strong desire to turn round and leave, and never return to this place. He stood still, afraid to turn the corner, knowing that if he took a few more paces there would be nothing at all between himself and his past. He was suddenly conscious of the utter smallness of his body, sensing the great sky above him and the earth beneath, the galaxy surrounding him, the universe beyond. He felt as though his body was supporting a great weight; or rather, as though his mind was supporting a psychological weight, much less tangible, but a million times heavier. He staggered forward a pace. Perhaps the sun was affecting his mind. He put up an arm to shield his eyes, deliberately walked on, and abruptly the oppressive feelings disappeared. He smiled to himself at the intrusion of his own imaginative proclivities at this particular moment when, after turning this bend in the drive, it would all be there before his eyes. He could see the front garden already, and could see that it was overgrown, a mass of nettles and brambles. A tree had been choked by ivy.

And now he could see it.

Even in the brilliant light of the afternoon sun the house presented a forbidding appearance. Although the front garden was no longer as he remembered it, and although the windows were broken, and part of the house obscured by the flank of a bright yellow bulldozer, the sight of it was still enough to fill him with a sense of unease, the feeling the house had always given him, and a kind of horrified nostalgia.

He had not seen the house for nine years. He was unable to explain to himself why he had come back here, when by this time next week the house would no longer exist. He had few happy memories of the lifetime he had spent here, and these were destroyed by the horror of his mother's death, and the family's precipitate departure after the compulsory purchase order.

The wall that had surrounded the front garden now lay in rubble among the thistles and the overgrown privet bushes. Although he wanted nothing more than to see the house reduced to a pile of rubble, yet he had the strong notion that in demolishing the house, the workmen would be destroying something of enormous importance that transcended the physical presence of the building; something that could never be created again. Perhaps it was that this house, in which he had spent his first fourteen years, represented his life, and that the workmen's tools would be destroying not only a building, but his childhood.

Despite the evidence of destruction, on this Sunday afternoon there was a feeling of peace over the whole scene. The decaying building looked as though it would continue to decay, finally dying a natural death and turning into an overgrown mound, being absorbed into the undergrowth, and becoming part of the countryside. It was strange to be standing here like this and seeing the house, its brickwork lit by the sun, its walls beginning to succumb to the ivy, hearing the birds singing in the trees; it had a feeling of calm that had never been in evidence while he was living there. Perhaps the tension had come, primarily, from his parents, who lived in a kind of truce of co-existence, a truce which concealed a strange mixture of hostility and compassion.

His earliest memory. His mother, not as she must have been then, but as he remembered her later—the drawn face of an old woman. She sits in a chair, her head resting on the back. He plays with a model car on the carpet at her feet. The lines of the pattern have become roads; a matchbox is a garage. She is wearing blue slippers. His father has come in from his special room —the one he is not allowed to enter.

"Marcia, where the hell are my papers?" A loud voice. An angry voice. He feels frightened.

"Which papers?" His mother's voice is very quiet.

"There was a green folder, with a large plan and some papers on top of it. What the hell have you done with it?"

"Oh those; I put those in your cupboard on the right."

"Why do you always feel it necessary to move my things?"

"I've got to clean up, haven't I?"

"Clean up? Clean up? I wouldn't mind so much if you *did* clean up! You haven't touched this place for I don't know how long. It's filthy. Filthy! There's dust an inch thick in my study. There's a sink full of washing-up. I don't know what's come over you lately; at one time you kept this place spick and span, now you don't seem to care about what kind of conditions we live in."

"I'm sorry, darling, I don't know what's wrong; I've been so tired lately."

"Tired? I'm tired too. Tired of trying to bring up a young child in a pig-sty." His father's voice suddenly becomes more gentle. "Look, why don't you go round and see the doctor in the morning? He'll be able to give you a tonic or something."

When his father leaves the room, he suddenly feels tears running down his face. He is taken up, and is surrounded by his mother.

"There, there, my darling Robin, don't cry. He doesn't really mean it."

He buries his face in her softness, and gradually his unhappiness gives way to warmth and pleasure.

Slates are missing from the roof. There is a slight smell of decay coming from the building. The lawn, once a neat oval in front of the house, is now a shapeless patch of wild grass and brambles. All over the front of the Georgian building, paint that was once white and is now a shade of greyish cream, is peeling in great swathes from the plaster. It is strange that at the period in the life of a building when time is most critical—the moment at which demolition has just begun—it should look so timeless. It was as if this house had always been here, and would remain for ever—an unalterable fact of existence, like a mountain or an ocean. He walks across the garden, brambles whipping at his legs, and stands before the front door.

His mother has gone away, and has been gone for ages. He feels very unhappy, as if he will never see her again. His brother, who sleeps in the room next to his, and who is nearly as grown-up as his father—a fourteen year old, nothing like a baby of five—has been very sad as well; he can tell. He is in bed, and Daddy comes up to see him. He can remember only a little of this conversation.

"She is very ill. She will be coming back here the day after tomorrow, but she's had a very serious operation, and she will have to spend a lot of time in bed. Now I don't want you to worry her in any way. She must have a great deal of rest, and I'm going to make sure she gets it. So you'll have to be very, very good."

"Why is Mummy ill? She hasn't done anything."

"People get ill; they don't have to be very bad."

"I think God is wicked to let Mummy be ill."

"Now don't say things like that. If we both pray for her as hard as we can, she may be quite better soon."

His father had left, and he had been very unhappy. Instead of saying his usual prayers that night he had said, "I hate you, God, for making Mummy ill, and I think you are very wicked. I'll kill you, God!"

The glass in the front door had been smashed, and now one could see through into the blackness of the hall. Inside, he could see dirty floorboards, and the broken plaster of the walls. Over one of the smashed panes there was a translucent spider web, moving gently in the air. Now he was so close the house looked much smaller than he remembered it. This gave him a feeling of security, a sense that his memories could no longer hurt him. He wondered again about his motives in coming here. On hearing that the council were at last going to go ahead with the main road, after an even longer than typical delay of nine years, he had felt an imperious summons to return here, as if it were essential that he have this final meeting with the house. As if, perhaps, he would learn something here, something he had never learned in all the years he had lived here.

He pushed open the front door, and it swayed in at a crazy angle, its top hinge no longer attached. The hat stand was still there, where it always had been; many things that his father had deemed useless had been left behind in their hurried, unnecessary departure. Even the mirror was still there, but it had been smashed, and broken pieces of glass littered the floor. He stepped inside the hall, conscious of the now-strong smell of damp plaster and decay. Bricks lay scattered all over the floor, and someone had written obscenities in bright red paint all over one of the walls. To the right the staircase still swept upward, but now many of the bannisters were missing, and he could see a hole in the tread of one of the steps. A piece of flex dangled down at the site of what once had been an elaborate light fitting and, in the corner, a piece of ceiling had fallen down, and now laths were exposed, like the ribs of the house's skeleton.

But it was only the surface that had shifted. All was basically the same. The stairs still curved round; the door to his left still indicated the lounge; another door further down on the right still concealed a large cupboard that filled the space under the staircase; the door at the end of the hall on the right was still the entrance of his father's study. He wondered why, then, he was not filled with the feeling of nostalgia that he had experienced so strongly when he had first caught sight of the house. Perhaps these small changes were enough to blunt the edge of his recollection. Perhaps the bricks littering the floor had at last broken the forbidding atmosphere of this building. There was one room he hoped had not changed; his mother's bedroom.

He is sitting on the sheet. "So we all waited for him down by the bridge, and then we got him and bashed him up!" She puts her head back and laughs, and then sweeps him against her.

"I know he is a bully, and he was fifteen and you're all only eight, but it's wicked to fight, and you mustn't anyway." She looks down on him. "Your face is too lovely for me to see it all cut and bruised." She touches the sore spot on his face.

"It's only a little bruise, and anyway he ran away."

She laughs again, and with his ear against her breast, he can hear the laughter rumbling in those great mysterious spaces inside her where, even now, he knows, a terrible disease is eating her away.

In that room he had seen her for the last time, with the face of an old hag, pieces of cotton wool stuffed into her nostrils, her flesh white and cold, and her face drawn into an expression that could have been a smile or a grimace of agony. But now he wanted to see the room for all the memories it had—not just to remember the times when she had looked younger, for he could only remember her as a woman made prematurely old by illness; in those earlier days he was sure that she had been beautiful—not to censor his memories, but to remember all, all the pain and unhappiness, so that he could stand and soak in the totality of what his mother had been.

He turned, and began to walk carefully up the stairs.

With the makeup removed, he could see that she was beautiful. And she was young, much younger than he had thought at first. Her face was oval, and gave a remarkable impression of serenity. She had large eyes, and the coloured light was reflected in her gaze as she looked at him intently. Her nose was straight, and it flared at the bottom into wide nostrils, which he could see were moving with the deep breaths she took. Her lips were full, but pale. Her face was full of paradoxes. It was a face that showed a deep sensuality, but at the same time a basic serenity of soul; it showed, in her high cheekbones and the set of her features, a great deal of strength, but at the same time a frightening frailty. She was young, but at this moment she seemed to be ageless, a monument, a figure of legend, as if time no longer had any meaning, as if her beauty could never fade.

A strong gust of wind set the lanterns swaying, and he watched the play of coloured light across the planes of her face. Everything he saw seemed to have an almost frightening significance, a meaning not usually attached to the mundane things of the world. Her dark hair, the swinging string of lanterns, the feel of the wind on his skin, a garden bench with a support broken in its back, the branches above them, moving slowly back and forth.

"I feel," he said slowly, breaking the long silence between them, "that in this garden there is—everything. As though all the time in the world has been gathered up here, and that this night will be an eternity for us."

"As though there is nothing," she said, her voice quiet, and almost drowned by the sighing of the leaves, "nothing at all in the world that can hurt us at this moment. That nothing exists apart from this moment. That we are the only breathing people in a world that is somehow our own world."

There was a gust of laughter from the house. Through the French windows he could see people moving about inside the brightly lit room.

"How old are you?" he asked, not believing that she had an age.

"My dear sir," she said, with an odd, halfhearted parody of primness, knowing that it was a question he had to ask, "that is hardly a polite question for a young lady to answer. But I'm nineteen."

"I'm twenty-three," he said. "I don't think I've ever seen anyone as beautiful as you."

"What are you called?"

"Robin."

"Robin. Robin. I love you, Robin."

"And I love you."

There was a tinkle of breaking glass from the house, and another roar of laughter. Reclining as they were on the grassy slope, their heads were turned toward each other, and her eyes were still fixed on his.

She spoke again.

"I feel that I ought to laugh at this strange conversation we're having. I've never spoken like this in my life before. It's as if it's hardly me that's speaking; as if I'm taking part in a play, and the whole scene is laid out before me. I ought to laugh, but at the moment I feel as though I won't be able to laugh again, ever."

As the French windows were opened, a flurry of conversation could be heard. He glanced up, and saw a group of people standing in silhouette outside the French windows, all carrying glasses in their hands.

"We can be seen from here," he said.

She looked up.

"He'll kill me if he finds us. Let's go further down."

He stood up and helped her to her feet. He could feel her warmth through the chiffon of her dress. He put his arm round her, and they walked down the slope into the darkest part of the garden. Here the light from the lanterns reached only faintly, and cast a pale glow on the far wall.

"Here is our place," she said, and she pulled back the branches of a thick bush, slipping through the space between the bush and the wall.

He could see, ahead of him, the skin of her back, the dim flesh touched with the pale colors of the lanterns' light, concealed at her waist, where the lines of her dress—begun at her shoulders by the straps—met, hiding her body from his view. He could see, beyond her, a little sheltered patch of grass, almost totally invisible from the lawn. He knew, as he began to follow her into the arbour, that he would never experience anything like this ever again . . .

He stood looking at the door of his mother's room. To the right, fungus was growing in a riot of orange along the skirting board, like the cancerous disease that had grown in his mother, until she could live no longer. He had been fourteen. It had been such a long disease. He remembered how, after she had died, he had been plunged into a world that seemed to have no meaning for him. When the wind blew in his face, it was a sensation of the skin. He was conscious of his eyes seeing, his ears hearing; it was as if the real person had curled up inside him, and was now far removed from the interpretation of these purely physical stimuli. It was a paroxysm of mourning, a mourning that had lasted for years. He was not sure that it was yet over.

Her blond hair was spread on the pillowcase, and the smell of her body was strong as he entered her. She wriggled beneath him, and he was conscious only of distaste, and of the rising muscular tension of his body. His spasms began and in his mind he counted them until his body was relaxed again. She lay quite still. He removed his penis, and carefully wiped it with his handkerchief. He looked at his watch.

"You're not," she said with heavy sarcasm, "exactly a Casanova, are you?"

In the alleyway he was suddenly conscious of the movements behind him. There were many of them.

There was still time for flight, but he couldn't be bothered. He turned.

There were four of them, large men, and they advanced threateningly. They had probably mistaken him for someone else. He stepped forward and was immediately plunged into a maelstrom of blows. He hit hard, not caring that he was being hurt as well. He kicked at someone's groin and heard a scream of pain. He felt something splinter under his fist, something else that was soft. And then there was a sudden release of pressure, and, abruptly, he was free. Three men were running down the alleyway. One man was lying on the ground clutching his crotch, moaning. He spat blood, and found a loose tooth with his tongue. There was blood dripping down from his face all over his clothes.

He was really quite badly hurt.

He spread his jacket out on the grass, and they sat down. There was now no more noise from the house; everything was still.

She spoke. "Do you mind if I have a cigarette?"

"No. Of course not."

She felt into her bag, brought out a pack of cigarettes and offered him one.

He refused the cigarette, but then reached forward and caught her arm, bringing the packet into a patch of light. "Minors? Do they still make those?"

"Oh, *don't!*" He too caught her distress, and he felt it as if a sudden cold wind had disturbed the warmth of the evening. She placed the cigarette in a long holder, lit it, and moved closer to him, so that he could feel her warmth. "What are we going to do about this, then?"

"This?"

"This *situation*. Are we going to make love here, and then go back to the party? Am I going to say to him, 'Darling, it's all off, I met a strange man in the garden and love him. Call off the party, there's no longer an engagement to have a party about.'? Are we going to make love here and then try to forget each other, and marry other people, and know that something forever will be missing from our lives? Or shall I go back to the party now, and try to forget that this ever happened?"

He spoke softly. "You can go back if you want to."

"You know that I can't."

He sighed, and lay down beside her. She shook her head, then stubbed out her cigarette on the grass, and lay back, inside the curve of his arm. The feel of her was electrifying. The flesh of her shoulders was enough to fill his body with an imperious erotic hunger. He leaned over her and looked down at her face. She was breathing deeply, and her eyes were liquid.

She put up a hand and stroked his face.

"Where have you come from?" she whispered. "You and your funny clothes. Why did you come? My life has been so simple up to now—I just don't know how to cope with this. Oh God, why did we have to meet like this?" She turned her head sharply away from him, and now he could see only her short dark hair, her ear, and a pulse throbbing in her neck. He put out a hand and gently pulled her head back. Tears were running down her face. He slowly lowered his face to hers, and found her lips with his own. He knew, as he felt the softness of her lips and the tip of her nervous tongue, that this night would be the high point of his life, and that after this, there would be nothing for him in the future . . .

He put out his hand to the door handle. He had to force the door open—over the years it had become warped—and then, on his right, he could see the bed. His mother's bed. The bed on which she had died, having refused point blank to enter a hospital, knowing that this was to be her death-bed. Now, after nine years, it stood at a crazy angle, although it was still in the position in which it had always been. He remembered his father going in and out of the room, especially during the last year, carrying trays of food, books for which she had asked, bedpans covered with a white cloth, or even the small cardboard box which apparently contained photographs of them together. During their engagement and wedding that, toward the end, she had asked for frequently. Despite their many arguments and rows, during the long and inexorable course of her illness his father had nursed her, if not with devotion, then with patience until, the day she lay dead in this bed, his duties had been completely discharged. Then a new briskness had come over him. They had gone, for a short while, to stay with an aunt, and then had moved to a flat in the suburbs of London. The three years he had spent in that flat had been almost intolerable. During the whole time he had felt nothing but a near-hatred for his father. All the time, he knew, he was blaming him for the death of his mother, and this feeling, while illogical, was powerful and grew more so, until he finally left, and went to live in a small flat in Kensington. The year after that his brother, then twenty-six, married, and his father was left to live alone. Now that the man was lonely and showing his age, he found it impossible to hate him any more and visited him every week. Now, the only reminders of the days of his mother's life were this house and this room.

She is lying back in the bed. He looks down at her face. It is thin, the face of a skeleton. Her skin is wrinkled and old, like the skin of an old woman, but with a yellow shade not normally seen in the flesh of living people. Her hair, gray and tangled, lies all over the pillow case.

He puts out his hand and strokes her brow.

"Oh, Robin, I've been thinking so much about you during the last few months. I've been worrying about certain things for years, and—

"You shouldn't worry, Mum, you know it's bad for

you. If you rest and take it easy, perhaps you'll be on your feet again one day."

"Oh, Robin, Robin, I wish you wouldn't humor me. Or yourself. I'm never going to be on my feet again. You know as well as I do that it won't be long before I die. I can accept it. You'd probably be surprised if you knew what a little thing death is for me. I've never clung to life—never felt it was worth clinging to. At least, not since I was a young girl."

"Oh, don't talk like that, Mum." There are incipient tears in his eyes, and he feels a sense of panic, as he does every time she speaks of her own death.

"Oh, I'm sorry, love." She reaches out and draws him close. She lifts up a hand, and gently runs it over his cheek.

"When I look at you I—Oh, Robin, if you only knew what I sometimes fancy to myself lying here . . . But it's just the ravings and flutterings of a dying woman's mi—"

She convulses in a spasm of pain, and a loud cry is forced from her. He feels his own face twisting too, in imitation of her agony. He quickly goes to the door of the room and calls, hearing his cry echoing through the house and echoing through his numb brain, as it has many times before.

"Dad! Dad! Come quick, she's in pain again!"

She is lying back on his jacket. He can see her face below in the shadows, illuminated by a single spot of light that filters through the leaves. Her face is given a pale phosphorescence, like the face of a Madonna. He lowers himself to her. They kiss with urgency, and he thrusts his body against hers. As his mouth travels the skin of her face, her ear, her neck, her shoulder, his hand pushing the shoulder strap down her arm, he feels overwhelmed by what he is experiencing, as if he is perpetually on the point of fainting. Her lips are moving

93

over his neck, and her hands run over his chest and back as if she were eagerly trying to trace the contours of a piece of sculpture. His hand finds the shape of her breast beneath the dress. He can feel the nipple clearly, and as it hardens under his fingers, he realises that she is not wearing a brassiere. He unbuttons her dress, lowers the shoulder straps, and uncovers the upper part of her body, as if he were helping a bud to blossom. They clutch each other, and now he can feel her flesh with his hands, his arms and his lips. She unbuttons his shirt, kissing his flesh with every button, lower and lower. He feels her thighs under the dress, and feels that she is wearing elaborate garters. He rolls her stockings down her legs, and then runs his hand back up to her thighs, hearing the catch in her breath. The backs of his fingers brush between her legs. Her hand is over his prick, and he is filled with an infinite sweetness. He has never known sensations like this before; it is as if their love-making has released a mechanism that until now has been still. Now the levers lift, the wheels spin, and the machine rolls off across the universe, tilted and crackling. He pulls the dress over her head, and sees that she is wearing long, wide, silk knickers. He laughs, his laugh like the humor of the cosmos, and pushes his head between her legs, rubbing his face all over the silk. And now, as he kisses her thighs, and feels the smooth surfaces of her bottom, drawing down the silk pants, he can feel her pulling his last remaining garment over his legs. Now they are both naked, and dimly he can hear the sound of a bird and muted noises from the house-party, but he is conscious only of her scented nakedness, of her hands moving on his flesh. He gently parts the lips of her cunt, and then lowers his mouth to the soft flesh, feeling, at the same time, her mouth, a sensation of such exquisite pleasure that it is almost beyond bearing. As his mind registers that she *is* in fact a virgin, and an answering thought expresses the part of his mind that knew this already, he is too busy to heed it, his frantic tongue travelling over the salty flesh in its quest and his quest to *know* her.

It is dark in his bedroom. There is very dim moonlight, but it serves only to change the room into a collection of frightening shapes. He can hear the tick of the big grandfather clock in the hall; a little while ago it struck eleven. He can also hear the voices of his parents. All day Mum and Dad have been angry with each other; they hadn't said anything bad, but it was easy to tell. He shivers in the bed. He doesn't like Dad shouting at Mum, especially as she's not been well for so long. Two years, what a long time to be ill! He wonders if she will always be ill, will always have to go to bed and rest in the afternoon, will always look so tired. His parents always seem to be angry with each other lately, and yet last year, when they said the war was over, he thought that everything would be all right from then on, and that they would always be happy, and that Mum and Dad wouldn't be angry with each other any more, and that Mummy would get well again. But here he was, hearing their voices raised in anger as he had so often before. He snuggled down in the bed, and tried not to listen. But the sounds they made were too intrusive, and he couldn't ignore them. He sometimes prayed to God when they shouted at each other, but God didn't make them stop, and he found that he didn't like God as much as he had when he'd been little. His stomach was twisted up again, and he would have to go alone to the lavatory. He swung his legs out of the bed, and dropped quietly to the floor. He put on his slippers and made his way across the room, taking care not to bump into the table, and opened the door. The landing was very creepy, lit as it was only by the stray light from downstairs, and he went as quickly as he could to the lavatory. Once inside he switched on the light and bolted the door, feeling much safer. It was then, as he was sitting there, that he had an idea. He remembered that as he had come along the landing the voices of his parents had been much clearer. If he were to go downstairs and sit on the staircase, he would be invisible from the lounge if the light was on and the door was open, and he would be able to hear what his parents were saying.

He wiped his bottom rather ostentatiously, pulled up his pyjamas, and then pulled the chain, making sure he was outside before the lavatory made that loud sucking noise. He could still hear his parents' voices, so they hadn't heard the sound of the lavatory.

He made his way back along the landing, and then, step by step, began to descend the staircase, trying hard not to make any creaking noises. Although the door of the lounge was shut, he could still hear the voices quite clearly. When he was nearly at the bottom of the stairs he stopped and listened. He heard his father's voice first.

"I've tried. I've tried, but what do you think it's like for me?"

"Can't you show me any kind of consideration at all?"

"I try to make allowances. I even try to retain some kind of emotional equilibrium over the children, which is more than you do. By all accounts I should hate Jack and love Robin, but I've tried not to be influenced by the past, and I try to think of Jack as my own son. I think I've succeeded. But you . . . I can't understand it. First of all it was Jack you were all over—he was the only one you cared about; Robin was just an unimportant interruption to you—"

"That's not true!"

"But now, now you've suddenly started turning all your maternal charms on Robin, and you're well on the way to turning him into some kind of pouffy mother's boy!"

"That's not true and you know it! And if you'd just try to understand how—"

"Understand? Understand? How many men would understand the fact that at the altar their bride was three months pregnant by another man?"

"Oh, we've been through all this so many times before! I *tried* to tell you, you know I did, but you wouldn't listen to me. And after that it was no use. I didn't care whether I married you or not; I just felt sorry for you."

"Understand. My Christ! And if it had been a proper affair it might have been a bit easier to understand. But it was a casual pick-up, wasn't it? A quick fuck in a bush."

"Oh, don't torture yourself with it! It was over fifteen years ago. You know there's never been anyone else since then. And if I've begged your forgiveness once I've begged it a thousand times. I know I was wrong. I know it was a terrible thing to do to a man. But what have I got to do? What can I do?"

"I'll never forget, as long as I live, one thing that summed up your whole stinking attitude. I agreed. All right, we would think of the child as ours, not as a result of his mother's fucking around. And then you told me what you were going to call him. You didn't even ask me! My God, are you surprised that I put my foot down? You're lucky I let you have your way with Robin; although why the name was so important to you I don't know, although I suspect. If my suspicions were correct I don't know what I'd do—but I don't want to think of that. What I am objecting—"

"Why? Why are you persecuting me like this?"

"Me persecuting you? Ha! If ever the day will . . ."

Robin didn't understand what his parents were saying to each other, but he vaguely got the feeling that they were angry at him and Jack, and he felt tears welling up in his eyes. Trying to choke back his sobs, so that his parents wouldn't hear him, he went quietly back upstairs and climbed back into bed.

He walked slowly out of his mother's room, and went back down the staircase, avoiding all the missing treads. Once in the hall he went toward the back of the house, stepping over piles of bricks, and trying to avoid the holes in the floor. The kitchen was a shambles, with the door no longer there, and broken glass all over the floor. The sink had been pulled away from the wall, and had been smashed into chunks of procelain. Now he was beginning to feel very depressed as all the changes really began to register with him. At that time his life had been bad—he had often been very unhappy—but still it had the kind of qualities that were so lacking in his existence today. He had come from a life of deep miseries but sudden joys, and was now in a strange flat land, a hinterland of the mind, in which the weather was always gray, the climate bland, and the population unimportant.

He went out of the kitchen entrance, into the back garden. He was horrified at the changes that had occurred here. He had always loved the garden, and had spent much of his time here, and he hated to see it in such a state of barrenness. The front garden had been overgrown and luxuriant, but here the predominant colors were brown and yellow. There was a terrace at the back of the house, and then a paved path led right down, almost the whole extent of the lawn. The lawn was now covered by scrubby grass and a few bushes. The path was uneven, and he walked carefully along it. The flower beds were almost indistinguishable from what had been the lawn; they now displayed nothing more than stringy nettles and yellow grass. The garden now had a depressing aspect once peculiar only to the house. The only things he really recognized were the metal lamp standards that flanked the path, some of which were by now very crooked, the fountain, past the end of the path, just before the lawn sloped down to the far wall, now dry and cracked, the garden bench on the right, and the little cherub statue at the end of the path. He patted the cherub's behind, as if in condolence.

By now it was impossible to convince himself that she had much more time to live. Death was written on her terrible face, lined with years of agony; death was written in the movements of her crabbed hands as they plucked and pulled at the sheets. It was there in the constant spasmodic pain, relieved only by frequent morphine injections; in the shouts and groans that she was no longer able to prevent.

Today she was very agitated. Her mouth quivered like the mouth of a senile old woman. There were egg-stains on her nightdress. She gabbled something at him, but he was hardly able to hear what she said now, and she dribbled saliva down her chin. He wiped her mouth, and said, "Just try to lie quietly, Mother."

She writhed on the bed in what looked like a parody of impatience, and then screamed briefly as she was struck by another convulsive wave of pain.

"Robin! Robin!" she was calling.

He hoped that she was not going to have a really bad spell. It was strange how one became so detached from someone in this condition. It was as if one could divide one's mind into compartments, so that his mother would be on one level, and this gibbering, scarcely human creature on another. Perhaps this was just a defence against the pain she was suffering. There was no pleasure at all in the life she had remaining; just a declining resistance to pain.

"Robin!" she called, only quieter this time. Her breath had been rasping very badly for the last two days, and now, it suddenly seemed to be much worse; it was as though she was having difficulty in breathing at all. He wondered if he should call his father. He made a move toward the door, and then was horrified to feel a hand clutching his arm. He looked back and saw that his mother was sitting up in bed looking at him with piercing eyes. He stifled the revulsion he felt at her clutching hand, and turned back to her. Was she looking at him, or was she looking rather at something in her own head? She had not been strong enough to sit up for months. What had happened?

"Robin," she said in a clear voice. "Robin, my darling, I love you." And then the hand tightened briefly, painfully before relaxing and falling away.

She had fallen back on the bed, her eyes still open, still with a strange, intent expression on her face.

She did not move.

He was in no doubt at all that she was dead.

To add the final indignity to her end, from under the sheets came the sound of a liquid fart.

She was dead.

She was dead.

He would never see her again.

Now he was filled with a desire to be in her; a desire that was pulling his prick toward her thighs, and a desire was in her that was thrusting her body toward him. He had wanted to prolong their lovemaking as much as possible, but they were no longer able to remain two. He lay on top of her, looking down at her face. He moved closer, touched, penetrated a fraction, and she winced. He remained still for a while, all the time with his eyes fixed on hers, knowing that his eyes were communicating the same message that he could read in her gaze. A little more, and she gave a small gasp of pain. He began to withdraw slightly, but her head turned from side to side. "No . . . no . . ." she said, and he felt her fingers digging into the flesh of his buttocks, urging him forward. He moved, in response to her fingers, and slid inside her, while she caught her breath and bit her lip. And he was there. This was where he belonged. It was just like coming home. He had never felt this with another woman, that here, in the soft wet spaces of her vagina, was the very place for which he had been made, that their bodies had been designed to fit together perfectly, as if once they had been one creature; a single unit, and that some time in the past they had been cruelly parted.

But now they were together, and they lay there quietly, looking into each other's eyes, feeling the sensations of each other's bodies, sensations that they had never experienced before.

"I think I am a virgin, too," he said.

He was to see her tomorrow; now, in bed, he was trying to visualise her face in his mind. But it was impossible. Nothing would come clear in his head; his thoughts were swirling like gas over a bog. Death was so cursory; he wished there was something he could do to express the numb dismay he felt at this moment, and to honor his mother's name. It was as if the world was due to end, and had not, and he was still here, but feeling as unsuited to life as a frog in a desert. Planets should have cracked, galaxies collapsed, the whole universe slid down a vortex and disappeared. But here he was, lying in bed, and the rest of his life was spread out before him like a long straight road, with featureless countryside on either side. Soon there was to be the funeral, a ludicrously inappropriate ritual, and then he would become one of those people who are obsessed by a small patch of ground; whose life revolves round the burial-place of the dead. But perhaps there was something he could do. Perhaps he could pay her his last respects in his own way, in his own words, not repeating the chanting doggerel of some priest.

He climbed out of bed, naked and shivering, and got into his dressing gown. He quietly opened the door of his bedroom, and stood listening intently. There was no sound from his father's room. He carefully moved out on to the landing, and then made his way quietly to his mother's room. He listened outside for a while, then opened the door and went in.

From now on the moment was ceremonial. Everything had become invested with a symbolic kind of significance. Every movement in the ritual must be slow; must be carried out with great delicacy and understanding. His every gesture must have some kind of ceremonial meaning.

Although he could see the vague shape of her on the bed, there was no sense of there being another person in the room. Apart from the sounds of his own body, the room was totally quiet. He walked slowly across the room and stood, for a moment, at the foot of her bed. Then he turned, and felt his way over to her dressing table. He felt for the handles of the top drawer, then slowly slid it open.

Inside were the things he knew he would find. A box of long, thin candles, some jewellery, and an ornate crucifix. He opened the box of candles, withdrew one of them, and lit it. The room was filled with a warm yellow glow. He walked across the room with the candle held high above his head, and then slowly placed it to one side of her headboard.

The men had been at her already. Pieces of cotton wool had been stuffed up her nose and into her mouth. Her cheeks were now rounded with a fake vitality that she'd never had in life. Her mouth was drawn into a horrible grimace. Here eyes were closed.

He walked with a slow tread back to the dressing table and lit another candle. There were now hardly any shadows in the room; all was bathed in a warm even light. He slowly walked across to her bed with the other candle held high, and then placed it carefully by the other side of the headboard. In the same way he positioned two more candles, one on either side of the foot of the bed. The bed was not lit by a bright illumination, and there were no shadows at all on her face. She looked like a bland effigy made from white wax. He knelt briefly by the side of her bed, and then stood up and went back to the dressing table. He picked up a cushion from a nearby chair, and placed it on the smooth top of the dressing table. From the jewel box he withdrew a glittering necklace. Holding it at arm's length, for a while he watched the smooth light of the candles as it was reflected a hundredfold in the facets of the little stones, to produce a ribbon of fire. Then he placed the necklace carefully in the center of the cushion, lifted cushion and necklace, and deliberately transferred them to a small table by the side of the bed. Then, bending forward, he briefly pressed his lips against the little string of jewels. He picked up the necklace again, turned, and laid it across the neck of his dead mother, shuddering at the feel of her stone-cold flesh. He was not able to fix it at the back, but tucked the loose ends in at the back of her neck, and arranged the necklace so that it appeared to be worn normally. He straightened, then turned, and walked back to the dressing table. From the jewel box he selected another necklace, and fixed it carefully and seriously round his own neck. Then he picked up the crucifix and, holding it in the palms of flat hands, he returned to his mother's side. He placed it on the cushion at the side of the bed. The bed had not been made for someone to be comfortable in, and the sheets were tucked in tightly; he loosened them, and folded back the sheets, so that her green nightdress was revealed down to the waist. He picked up the crucifix, and reverently placed it between her breasts, then bent again, and gave it a lingering kiss. Then he rose, and moved slowly round to the foot of the bed. He knelt, closing his eyes.

Now he felt that in some way he was in communion and warmth. The candles had given the room a sense of intimacy, suggesting by their yellow light, that there was nothing at all outside the room, that nothing else existed. He mumbled words to her, not prayers, but words of love, memories and dreams. The moment was hushed and magical.

But as he spoke he felt a sudden stirring in his groin, and a wave of his imperious adolescent sexuality. His words faltered into silence, and he felt for a moment horrified, as if he had violated a church. But then, as he looked at the room, the jewels, the corpse, the ceiling, yellow with the candles' light, he realised that it was all right, that it fitted, and he allowed it to go on, permitting himself to be washed by these powerful waves, his hands going nervously to his erect penis. He took off the dressing gown, and stood naked at the foot of her bed. His body was quivering, and his hand moved back and forward in the rhythms of sex, his eyes fierce, and his lips whispering to her. He leaned forward, as if in torment, and with one hand supported himself on the footboard of the bed, which in turn began to shake slightly, the jewels at her neck sparkling with this movement. And then his face was twisted with the waves of an ecstasy that he had never felt before, and he had to bite his lips to prevent himself from crying out, and as he came, in a great wash of colors, and as the young semen fell in drops on to the bed, he kept his eyes, all the time, on her.

The trees did not have many leaves, even though it was the height of summer; it was as though a strange blight had fallen on the garden, and living things now avoided this place. He took his hand from the cherub, and looked back toward the house. He was mesmerised by it; it was impossible to take his eyes away. It seemed that the longer he stayed here, the more meaning the house seemed to have for him. The picture of the building as it was, half-decaying, and illuminated by the afternoon sun, was totally compelling. The house was gaining, every moment, a strange kind of importance, as if here was the vortex of a field of forces, and the bricks were sucking into themselves a vast amount of a totally intangible material. He had a sudden feeling of being very close to his past. The house in his memory seemed as close as the house he was now watching. There was a flash of darkness in front of his eyes. He was beginning to get imaginative again. He deliberately cleared his mind of thoughts.

He could see the terrace, the French windows, the kitchen, the upper story with the great bay windows and, in the roof, the smaller windows of the attic. The roof was very red. The pattern of the tiles reminded him of the patterns of electronic circuitry, and he could imagine the roof alive, crawling with strange forces. A flash of darkness in front of his eyes. He saw that in a way the house could never really be destroyed, for it was a little part of the universe, as wide as that, as high as that, as deep as that, as old as that, and in that section of time it would exist always. A flash of darkness. He looked at the roof, and in its patterns he suddenly found a truth that he had never seen before. He knew that he had learned something from that red tile, from the whole house, that would have been unimaginable before. Darkness. Light again. He sensed that the house was not the object that he now saw, but a form, a perfect form, that stretched through the cold winds of time. Darkness—lights within the darkness. Light. And suddenly he could see that the darkness he was intermittently seeing, was just another aspect of this summer light. Darkness—lights. Daylight. That the sky, when it became dark, was just another aspect of itself that he had been unable to see before now. If one holds a photographic negative over a dark surface in such a way that the light is striking it at an acute angle, sometimes the image can be seen as a positive one, and yet, at the saem time can be understood as a negative. Darkness— colored lights—house—stars. Daylight. The periods of darkness were becoming more frequent and longer, but he knew that it was just a matter of his own perceptions, with her, and his closeness gave him a sense of comfort and that the light sky he kept seeing was, in a sense, just an aspect of this night, just a subtle shifting of perspective. Light. The night again. He tried not to allow too many thoughts to enter his mind, and just to experience these perceptions. He sensed that too much thought could be dangerous. Light. The night again. But the flashes of light were becoming less frequent, and shorter, the night was drawing in again. He could see the stars, and he looked at these, waiting for this strange time to pass. A flash of light. The stars were cut off where the roof of the house was silhouetted against the sky. A flash of light in front of his eyes. He could hear a cricket singing from somewhere in the distance, but as he listened for it, the sound ceased. Now he could hear only the trickling of the little fountain. With the light shining from the French windows, and the people moving about inside, with radiance cast on the terrace, the house looked quite beautiful. The scent of blossom was heavy on this July night, and he drew in a deep breath and looked round, at the trees, at the lanterns strung on wires running between the lamp standards, and at the house. He began to walk slowly about the garden.

And as he watched her face beneath him, he began, slowly, to move. And he felt the world moving with him, the garden, the blossom, the trees, all taking part in this vast act of love. She moaned, beneath him, and he felt his movements to be part of the universe, part of the gigantic mechanism, the enormous clock, its wheels as big as a galaxy. And as he moved in her time passed without either of them being aware of it, but both sensing the movement of the stars, planets, continents, people, atoms, in the movements their bodies were making. He felt as though he were taking part in a ritual dance, and that each movement that they both made was recorded somewhere in an enormous tome, in pages of minute symbols. He was now moving faster, and the

106

sense of plunging into her body caused him to shake and moan, as also she was convulsed and crying out, and their hips, twisting and plunging, were moving of their own volition, their vibrations making a sound, a song, the song of the stars.

And then he heard a door opening at the back of the house, and saw a young woman standing outside the kitchen entrance. She was wearing a long evening dress, and was carrying a glass. She stepped out on to the terrace and looked up at the sky. There was something about her that was strangely familiar; something about the set of her body, her attitude, and even from this distance he found her compellingly attractive.

And then she caught sight of him, and began to walk down the garden path toward him. As she got nearer and nearer, as he saw her body moving under the green dress, as her face became clearer, he began to breathe more deeply, wanting to take her in his arms, feeling a desire he had never felt for any other.

She stood in front of him, looking up at him. Her dress, he could now see, was a very pale green, with a V neck and shoulder straps. She was wearing a simple necklace. Her hair was short, cropped, with a curl curving forward under each ear.

When she spoke her voice was slow, serious and wondering.

"Who are you?"

"I . . . I . . . nobody . . . I don't know." Just who was he? He spoke again. "Who are *you*?"

"I . . . I can't tell you. I feel that I shouldn't tell you. Please don't ask me to."

Her face was heavily made up, but he could see her large dark eyes, and the shape of her features, and knew that she was very lovely. The colored lanterns moved above their heads, and the changing colors emphasized her attractiveness.

The garden was absolutely still.

"What a strange meeting!" he said.

She smiled.

"You feel what I feel, don't you?"

He nodded.

"I don't know how I know; I just do."

"We seem to know everything about each other," he said. "It's as though we are closer to each other than any two people have ever been before."

"I think we are going to make love."

"Yes."

"I am a virgin, you know. I've never been with a man before."

"This is so strange."

"Oh God, what will happen? I'm going to be married soon. That is what this party is all about. I suddenly don't know whether I love him or not."

"I would like to see you without makeup. Can we take it off?"

She nodded, and moved toward the little fountain. He watched her as she bent over and washed her face, and as he looked at her slim form it seemed to him that her body was at once familiar and strange. He handed her his handkerchief, and she dried her skin. He walked further along the garden, to the slope where the lawn inclined down to meet the far wall, and after a few moments she joined him, lying down beside him, smiling.

With the makeup removed, he could see that she was beautiful. And she was young, much younger than he had thought at first. Her face was oval, and gave a remarkable impression of serenity. She had large eyes, and the colored light was reflected in her gaze as she looked at him intently. Her nose was straight, and it flared at the bottom into wide nostrils, which he could see were moving with the deep breaths she took. Her lips were full, but pale. Her face was full of paradoxes. It was a face that showed a deep sensuality, but at the same time a basic serenity of soul; it showed, in her high cheekbones and the set of her features, a great deal of strength, but at the same time a frightening frailty. She was young, but at this moment she seemed to be ageless, a monument, a figure of legend, as if time no longer had any meaning, as if her beauty could never fade.

A strong gust of wind set the lanterns swaying, and he watched the play of colored light across the planes of her face. Everything he saw seemed to have an almost frightening significance, a meaning not usually attached to the mundane things of the world. Her dark hair, the swinging string of lanterns, the feel of the wind on his skin, a garden bench with a support broken in its back, the branches above them, moving slowly back and forth.

"I feel," he said slowly, breaking the long silence between them, "that in this garden there is—everything. As though all the time in the world has been gathered up here, and that this night will be an eternity for us."

"As though there is nothing," she said, her voice quiet, and almost drowned by the sighing of the leaves, "nothing at all in the world that can hurt us at this moment. That nothing exists apart from this moment. That we are the only breathing people in a world that is somehow our own world."

There was a gust of laughter from the house. Through the French windows he could see people moving about inside the brightly lit room.

"How old are you?" he asked, not believing that she had an age.

"My dear sir," she said, with an odd, halfhearted parody of primness, knowing that it was a question he had to ask, "that is hardly a polite question for a young lady to answer. But I'm nineteen."

"I'm twenty-three," he said. "I don't think I've ever seen anyone as beautiful as you."

"What are you called?"

"Robin."

"Robin. Robin. I love you, Robin."

"And I love you."

There was a tinkle of breaking glass from the house, and another roar of laughter. Reclining as they were on the grassy slope, their heads were turned toward each other, and her eyes were still fixed on his.

She spoke again.

"I feel that I ought to laugh at this strange conversation we're having. I've never spoken like this in my life before. It's as if it's hardly me that's speaking; as if I'm taking part in a play, and the whole scene is laid out before me. I ought to laugh, but at the moment I feel as though I won't be able to laugh again, ever."

As the French windows were opened, a flurry of conversation could be heard. He glanced up, and saw a group of people standing in silhouette outside the French windows, all carrying glasses in their hands.

"We can be seen from here," he said.

She looked up.

"He'll kill me if he finds us. Let's go further down."

He stood up and helped her to her feet. He could feel her warmth through the chiffon of her dress. He put his arm round her, and they walked down the slope into the darkest part of the garden. Here the light from the lanterns reached only faintly, and cast a pale glow on the far wall.

"Here is our place," she said, and she pulled back the branches of a thick bush, slipping through the space between the bush and the wall. He could see, ahead of him, the skin of her back, the dim flesh touched with the pale colors of the lanterns' light, concealed at her waist, where the lines of her dress—begun at her shoulders by the straps—met, hiding her body from his view. He could see, beyond her, a little sheltered patch of grass, almost totally invisible from the lawn. He knew, as he

110

began to follow her into the arbor, that he would never experience anything like this ever again. . . .

They moved together violently, their loving now the only fact of the universe. There was nothing except each other, and they moved like a single creature.

Their violence in love was a kind of tenderness. It was a total freedom which they had given each other, a total trust. He could no longer feel the summer night; he could feel only her body, his body, he could hear only the sounds they made. Their movement, too, was a kind of stasis, a still eternity of sensation, as though they were both suspended in space, and nothing was happening, nothing was moving.

But the dance was coming to its conclusion. He was conscious of a growing sweetness, communicated from her, as her head began to move from side to side, and he heard the regular moans coming from her throat.

The feelings grew, widened, became a field of white, an iridescent snowscape, and she began to cry out, and he was falling into a void, seeing her face expressing her sweet agony, and then there was nothing but whiteness in his brain, and he dimly heard his own cries, and a scream which was torn from her. And then nothing but the surges, and, for a moment, he felt that he was her and she was him, and throughout the whistling void of time they would never be parted.

And then they were still.

This moment after was like death, and they were still sharing this, having come through the storms together.

Her face was totally blank. She looked as though there was no more life within her.

And as he lay in her, he began to be conscious again of the passing of time, and as each minute went by, it was one minute less of the time they had remaining. And he knew that there were not many minutes left.

As if she sensed this, she opened her eyes, and gazed deeply at him.

"Oh darling!" she whispered.

And it was nearly over. He knew that he would have to get up and put on his clothes, for the time was almost run out. He withdrew from her, feeling a terrible sense of loss, and knowing, by the movement of her eyes, that she felt this too. He stood up.

"Perhaps," she said, still lying in an attitude of abandon, "this has ruined my life. It will certainly affect my whole future. And yet I know that as long as I live, I will never regret this."

As he dressed, he looked at her.

"I know. If I never live again, at least I lived tonight in a way I never have before."

And as he put on his jacket, he knew that he had to walk back to the cherub. He stood looking at her for the last time, as she lay with her arms and legs outspread, like a fallen statue. The swinging of the lanterns made her body seem to be moving gently, an echo of their love-making. The bushes stirred in a soft breeze. There was a flash of light.

"I've got to go now," he said.

Her eyes opened wide.

"I know," she said.

He began, slowly, to walk backward away from her, keeping his eyes fixed on hers. He could see that she was crying.

"Oh God, Robin," she called, "I hope I'm pregnant. I hope to God I'm pregnant!"

The branches of the bush were now beginning to hide her body from his view. A flash of light. But he could still see her face.

"Good-bye, my darling," he said.

A last branch swung into place, and cut off the communion of their eyes. He felt as though a vital organ had been torn from his body.

As he walked back to the cherub, through the flashing lights of his mind, he heard her voice for the last time.

"Robin, my darling, I love you!"

The sun seemed intolerably hot. He was half-blinded by the light, which was reflected by the tears in his eyes. He walked over the parched earth, conscious of the wetness running down his face, and sat on the old garden bench, the one with the support broken in its back. He took out his handkerchief, and rubbed savagely at his eyes, but he was unable to suppress the sobs he was making. The bush, whose branches he had just pushed through, was now black and small, and the luxuriant foliage had totally disappeared. Now he could see past it into the arbor. Now there was nothing but soil covered by patches of weed.

He dried his eyes and looked up at the house. No longer charged with significance, it appeared to him as it had when he had arrived.

There was a bird singing nearby.

His mind was a maze, but he knew that one day he would have to piece together all the complex implications of what had happened. Now, he could only mourn, as he had mourned her once before.

Had she known, at the end? As she lay dying, and watched her second son growing older and gradually taking on the appearance of her brief lover, did she think it was a matter of coincidence, and nothing else?

He began weeping again, his body shaking on the bench. Life now, after this day, seemed to be intolerable. But he would have to live. Soon he would leave, and go back to his home in London. If he ever came this way again he would be driving in a car or a coach, along the road over the place where the house had been. And perhaps he would not know its exact location, and would not be able to sense just when the wheels of the vehicle would be running above the site of this house and this garden. And perhaps he would not care; perhaps the hold that the house, his past, his family, and his lover had over him would, from now on, be broken forever.

But even as he thought this, he knew that it was the opposite of the truth.

Foreword to SURFACE IF YOU CAN

Terry Champagne is a young writer, and "Surface If You Can" is her first work of speculative fiction. She is typical of the new kind of speculative writer only in her very atypicality. Where most of the traditional science fiction writers have been narrow specialists, Terry Champagne, like several of the new speculative writers, considers speculative fiction only one aspect, perhaps even a minor aspect, of her total creative concern. Still under twenty-five, she has been writing a regular column of opinion on eroticism and social questions as well as fiction, and is a photographer, sculptor, and painter of considerable accomplishment. She has also danced professionally and engaged in a few semi-shady operations. Exotic as all this may sound, and in fact may be, it is not all that atypical of the range of sensibility which many new writers are bringing to speculative fiction.

"Surface If You Can" brings a new approach to sexual explicitness to speculative fiction. For Terry Champagne, as for a few others, the issue of how much is permissible no longer exists; it is a dead letter, it is already decided, and the criterion is simply to write what comes naturally. Good taste is no longer an issue, for this kind of unself-conscious honesty transcends taste and makes it meaningless. "Surface If You Can" is not a story that points to its own daring like a naughty little boy. It's a good story, honestly written, that deals with its various elements seamlessly. At turns tragic and grossly funny, subtle and broad, nasty and tender, it's life and life only.

SURFACE IF YOU CAN

by Terry Champagne

Mrs. Amis felt a need. In spite of her health and wealth and elaborately equipped Bel Air mansion, she wanted to do-give-get something. So she placed an ad in the newspaper of the closest overcrowded university.

For Rent. Conv. bmb. sheltr., furn., util. pd., priv. estate, Bel Air, cpl. pref., $95., ph. 273-5840.

Pam and Allan met in a restricted, upper class poetry writing class. Pam's sophomoric standing as an art major proved no barrier when she impulsively registered for the class, despite lack of all prerequisites. Poetry was her passion—along with art, music, ballet and Renaissance architecture. She was a beautiful person.

When she looked at Allan, she melted inside herself and a trenchant warmth fell between her legs. She could tell instantly that he was a beautiful person. Tall and broad and narrow, with heavy brown eyes, the jewels of his depths.

She admired his sensitivity and style. He admired her brightness, originality and trim, rounded body.

They said they would be right over, so Mrs. Amis watched for them. By the time they had walked to the door, she knew they were just right.

"Hello," she smiled, "I'm Mrs. Amis."

After they were all pleased to meet each other, Mrs. Amis said, "But I'm sure you're anxious to see the shelter."

They followed Mrs. Amis down a hall, into a massive game room, through tinted sliding glass doors, across a stone terrace skirting the pool, and onto an expanse of well-kept lawn which stretched to distant trees that obscured the wall.

As they walked, Mrs. Amis asked, "Are you both students at the university?"

"Yes."

"And what subjects are you majoring in?"

"English lit," said Allan.

"I'm majoring in art," said Pam, "but I may switch to English."

"How lovely," replied Mrs. Amis. "And where do your parents live?"

Allan replied first. "They used to live in Pasadena, but when I started school here, they bought a house in Huntington Beach. They live there now."

"My folks are in Thousand Oaks," Pam said.

(Thousand Oaks is one of the many communities which service a part of the vast tract that makes up Los Angeles' suburbia. The only unique thing about Thousand Oaks is that it is located in Ventura County.)

"Well, here we are." Mrs. Amis bent down to the cement encased hatch and drew it open. "Follow me," she said as she descended the steep, stairlike ladder, down into a dark well. At the bottom, she fumbled a few moments till she found the light switch.

Allan and Pam stood on the dark blue, deep pile wall-to-wall carpeting at the foot of the stairwell, and gazed around the room. The only furniture was a huge divan which matched the carpet and a long, low hatch-cover coffee table which had been painted white to match the smooth, white concrete walls and ceiling. The thirty-five foot length of the left wall was entirely taken up by built-in shelves, cabinets and wardrobes, all painted white with blue trim. At the far end of the room was a small, fully equiped kitchenette with matching decor.

"The couch folds out into a king size bed and there's a folding table in the kitchen. Over here (opposite the kitchenette, next to the stairs) is the toilet." She opened the door of a tiny cubicle containing a toilet bowl.

"It's only a chemical toilet," she continued, "but it's quite adequate. You'll have to do all your bathing in the kitchen, though."

They all wandered back to the living area. Pam looked at it all again. "We can really use all this storage space," she said. Then she noticed a row of meters in the wall. "What are these dials for?"

Mrs. Amis tried to remember. "This first one measures the outside radiation. I can't remember what it's called. And these others, I think, are connected to the air and water purification systems. It's been so long." She seemed lost in thought or reminiscences, but eventually she continued. "You know, if there ever is an attack, the hatch seals automatically and keeps you safe and sound until the radiation is gone. Then the two of you could return to the land and begin the race anew. You're such a lovely couple."

They mumbled their thank yous.

"This is just perfect," Pam said. "And it has so much character." She looked up at Allan.

"We'll take it," he said.

"Wonderful. I'm so happy I can do something to help

you young people. Education is so important. You kids today are the hope of the future."

How fresh and fertile young Pam looks, she thought as she watched them go. And how strong and manly her husband looks. Why, his long, thick hair makes him look even more virile. What a beautiful couple.

Shortly after Pam and Allan moved in, the cockroaches moved in. They knew that Pam and Allan weren't any more beautiful than any other people. It wasn't long before the cockroaches ventured out of the piles of boxes of books, papers and art supplies.

Pam arrived home before Allan on Monday afternoon. She dumped the stuff she was carrying on a pile of other stuff, adopted a cheerful wifely mien and walked toward the kitchenette. There was a sinkful of unwashed dishes which she filled with sudsy water and left. While the dishes soaked, she bent down and opened the tiny refrigerator. The steak and mushrooms she had planned for dinner last week were still there. Along with some milk and eggs, a dab of butter, a large wilted head of lettuce, a few cherry tomatoes and prunes, and half a chocolate bar. In the freezer were two boil bags containing corn and French green beans, and an almost-full half-gallon of the world's worst ice-cream which she hadn't gotten around to throwing out yet. She took a few tomatoes and a piece of chocolate, shut the door and walked to the end of the counter. There, she opened a decanter marked Tea and rolled a joint which she set aside to share with Allan later. Then she sat down at the kitchen table with the tomatoes and the chocolate and last week's *Free Press* which she hadn't gotten around to reading.

When Allan came in, Pam put down the newspaper and walked to him. He started to dump his books on the open, un-made sofa-bed, but pushed aside a pile of debris on the coffee table and placed them there instead.

"Hi."

"Hi."

They embraced. He pulled her down, beside him, on the bed.

"I rolled a joint. I'll go get it." She rose.

She returned with joint, matches and ashtray. While they were smoking, they spoke in strained stage whispers, trying to keep the smoke down at the same time.

"How was your day?" she asked, handing him the joint a little bit smaller.

He took a drag and replied, "Great!" He took another shorter toke and continued, "After class today, Horrison asked me what my plans were, where I was going to grad school. He already knows I'm staying here. Anyway, it turns out he wants me on his staff of TA's next quarter." He took another quick puff and offered it to Pam.

She sucked in a lungful of heavy smoke that permeated every cell of her body. When she spoke, her voice was in another world. "Teacher's Ass. Are you proud of that?" She handed him the half-smoked joint.

This time, he replied before he dragged. "Someone has to do it. It might as well be me, because I'll do a damn good job of it. I am planning to go into education, you know." He took a hearty drag and gave her the rest.

She took a small mechanical puff. "I'm sorry, Allan. I didn't mean to attack you, personally. I just hate classes where you only see the teacher once a month and he never sees you. I know you'll make a fantastic teaching assistant. I just wish that job weren't necessary." she looked down at the roach, took a quick, tiny puff and handed it to Allan.

He took as long a drag of the hot roach as he could. "Be careful. We could all, quite easily, be automated into obsolescence."

120

Micronite filter.
Mild, smooth taste.
For all the right reasons.
Kent.

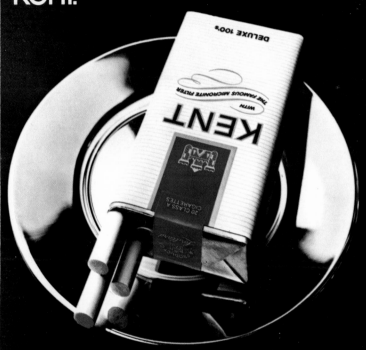

America's quality cigarette.
King Size or Deluxe 100's.

Kings: 17 mg. "tar,"
1.1 mg. nicotine;
100's: 19 mg. "tar,"
1.3 mg. nicotine
av. per cigarette,
FTC Report Aug. '72.

They smiled. She noticed the size of the joint and said, "Do you want me to get the roach clip?" Ready to rise.

He put his hand on her shoulder and said, "No, I'm stoned."

"So am I," she said.

He put the roach out in the ashtray, put the ashtray and matches on the table and drew her close to him. They kissed and petted slowly and slowly he unbuttoned her lacy blouse.

When they were naked, they rolled around for a while listening to the sounds of skin touching. She rolled onto her stomach with her arms dangling over the edge of the bed. He rolled gently on top of her, resting himself in the soft, warm crack of her buttocks, and slipped his hands under her to cradle her breasts.

When she was squirming slightly and breathing heavily, he moved into position and worked his way inside. Moved his hips and hands, heavier and heavier, moaning.

Pam screamed, a shrill startled scream. She squirmed and bucked frantically, crying out in agony.

Allan kept pushing, harder and harder, as he came. Make it last, he thought.

She kept squirming and moaning long after Allan was satisfied, but he wanted her to come, too, so he kept on as long as he could, until he collapsed on top of her.

She continued to writhe and cry beneath him.

He tried to stroke her hair, but she was in a rage. He rolled off.

The instant she was free of his weight, Pam leapt up and ran to the kitchen sink, sobbing.

Allan looked down at the mutilated cockroach body on the sheet where she had been. He went to her. She was rubbing her body with a wet washcloth and crying. He took her in his arms.

"I'm sorry," he said. "I didn't know about the cockroach."

She sobbed heavily and held him tighter. "I know," she said, "I know." She paused to sniffle. "It was so awful. I couldn't get away." She sobbed some more, but continued. "All of a sudden I could feel it wriggling between my breasts. That's when I screamed." She sniffled again. "I kept trying to get up. One time I got up high enough to see it, but then I fell onto it. I could feel it mash against my chest." She renewed her sobbing.

Allan held her and comforted her. "Poor baby, it's all over now."

Eventually, Allan sat her down and went to clean up the bed. He pulled out all the corners of the bottom sheet, folded one over the bug and rolled the sheet into a ball with the body of the dead cockroach at the centre. This he deposited in a heap near the stairs.

They dined on cookies and milk and later a second course of scrambled eggs. They sat around talking and smoking till very late, when they turned out the light and went wearily to bed. There, they made very, very gentle love and fell asleep.

During the night, something jarred them into halfa-wakened fear. They touched each other and muttered, thickly, groggily, incomprehensibly, and went back to sleep.

The alarm rang. One of them reached over and shut it off. Both of them knew it was set a quarter or a half an hour fast, so neither of them made an effort to rise.

By this time it was really late, they were running around frantically. Finally, they chased each other up the stairs.

"Wait a minute," Pam said, "I forgot my perfume." She ran back down the stairs.

Allan pushed up on the hatch. It didn't budge. He pushed again harder.

"Hey, I can't get the door open." Puzzlement and caution in his voice.

122

Pam watched his efforts to open the hatch. Unconsciously, she turned her eyes to the dials they had stopped noticing.

"Allan, this meter reads 6000."

Allan descended a few steps and looked at her.

"Mrs. Amis said this meter measures the outside radiation." She wanted to say more, but her voice vanished.

"Do you remember hearing an explosion last night?" he asked, as if it were the most important question ever asked.

"Yes, it felt like an earthquake."

"I sure wish we had bought that radio."

"I wish we had a window. I just can't believe it."

"I wish we had more food."

Before they could ponder their situation, and long before they could accept the reality of it, a shock wave jolted everything inside the shelter. They clung together.

"What was that?"

"Probably a second wave attack—or, maybe, their doomsday bombs," he replied.

"It still doesn't seem real," she said, distantly.

"Well, it is," he said. "Come on, we've got a lot of stuff to do."

But it didn't take them very long to enumerate their meager supply of rations.

The next day, when the alarm rang, they awoke with a start. Though there was no longer any reason to get up, they were already too hungry to go back to sleep. They spent a long, dull and discomforting day and after that, they no longer set the alarm. There was very little to keep them occupied during their waking hours, so they slept as much as possible.

Pam woke first, but lay as still as she could for as

long as she could, to forestall the eventual day. Allan woke and did the same until they became aware of each other's wakefulness and were forced to move. She rose first and went to the john. When she returned, she dressed, as usual, in a loose blouse and blue jeans. While Allan was in the head, she went to the kitchen, set some water on to boil, took a well-used teabag from the refrigerator and dipped it in the boiling water. When the water began to change color, she squeezed the moisture out of the teabag and returned it to the refrigerator. They breakfasted on this weak tea and their last two cookies. They ate slowly.

"These are the last of the cookies," she said.

"I know."

"Did you sleep well?" she asked, halfheartedly eager for conversation.

"Sure, the hungrier I get, the better I sleep."

Silently, they nibbled at their cookies and sipped their tea. Allan broke the silence.

"You gonna paint today?" he asked casually.

"Yeah," she replied, dully. "You're going to read?"

"Mmhmm. After I finish this book, I might do a little writing."

Eventually, lethargically, she picked up their teacups and rinsed them in the sink. He sat at the kitchen table and read; she moved to the other end of the room, near the stairs, where she kept her art materials in a large heap on the floor.

The morning passed. The time passed. They waited for one o'clock, when they could eat lunch. As the time approached, their eyes met more frequently as they turned to look at their clock.

For lunch, they ate ice cream: a hideous fudge-ripple ice cream that tasted like rubbing alcohol, which they were glad to have.

"Oh, Allan," Pam moaned, "the absolute, dead silence in here is driving me crazy. Do you think we can go up soon?"

"Not until the meter is back to normal," he said calmly and firmly. Subject closed. "Did you finish your painting?"

"Yeah. But it's not very good. I found some old drawings of mine from high school that're much better."

"Maybe you can dig through some of those boxes of shit in the closet and find some interesting stuff. We can redecorate again."

Their voices had become quiet monotones.

Later, Pam's shrill, but stifled, scream pierced the silence.

"What's the matter?" Allan asked, startled, as he walked toward her.

She was standing now, away from her fear.

"It was a cockroach." Before Allan could deride her for her stupid fear, she continued. "I was looking through an old scrapbook and it jumped out. I wasn't expecting it." She went to him and held him tightly, pressing close to him. "Allan, I'm so afraid."

He knew she wasn't just kvetching about the cockroaches and he held her tighter.

They moved to the bed. He stroked her hair and kissed her lightly, gently, on the mouth and forehead. He began to unbutton her blouse, she finished for him. They stood up and undressed themselves quietly.

Back on the bed, they touched each other languidly and moved scarcely at all. They made love slowly and gently and slowly and gently till Allan finally came, slowly, gently.

Even the small effort of making quiet love tired them. They rested in each other's arms hoping for sleep.

Pam worked frenetically, quietly as possible, whimpering all the while, to herd the scurrying roaches away from her and off her belongings. She had uncovered a horde of them living in a box she was exploring. Suddenly, Allan loomed up behind her, grabbed her shoulders and jerked her harshly from the scene of battle.

"Get out of there," he said, severely, as he pulled her away. "And keep quiet." He poured out the contents of the box and proceeded to stomp on every roach he saw. A few fast and lucky ones managed to scurry to safety under one of the other available piles of rubble.

"You'd better start getting used to them," he said when he had finished, "because we're going to have to start eating them soon" (or each other).

Pam was very silent while she cleaned up the mess.

The day their food was scheduled to run out, they sat very still and hungry in their respective corners of the room. The morning dragged. Finally, Allan, who couldn't see the clock and couldn't stand the suspense, asked, "What time is it?"

Pam looked at the clock and rose, saying nothing.

"What time is it?" he asked more impatiently.

"I don't know," she almost whispered.

"What do you mean?" he asked flatly as he rose.

"It stopped."

"Why?" he demanded on his way over to the bed where she and the clock were. "When was the last time you wound it?"

"I don't remember," she stammered, frightened. "I think yesterday at lunch."

"Stupid bitch."

"I'm sorry."

"What the fuck good does that do!" he screamed at her.

Enraged, he gripped her above the elbows, shook her and threw her onto the bed. Before she could move, he straddled her hips and pushed her shoulders into the mattress. She screamed the few obscenities she knew at

126

him and scratched his arms, ripped his shirt and tried for his face.

He let go her arms and she flayed at him as he removed his shirt and threw it on the floor. She fought him as he tried to unbutton her blouse, so he ripped it open, grabbed her wrists and bent over to bite her nipples, to ravage and caress every part of her with his tongue and teeth.

She stopped struggling and began to push and press her body toward him. He let go of her wrists and held her head while he pushed his tongue deep into her mouth. Her hands worked frantically to unfasten his pants.

He sat up, undid her jeans and pulled them off. Then he stood up on the bed over her and removed his own.

He dropped to his knees and bent to chew her nipples again. She screamed and raked her nails, hard, down his back. She pushed her hips up to him and dug her nails into his buttocks, forcing him down on her.

Once they were locked together, they strangled each other in grips of arms and legs, writhed violently and bit each other savagely for a short time. They came one right after the other.

Thoroughly exhausted, they slept for an unknown period of time.

When they woke, they were hungrier than ever. Slowly, they rose and went to the kitchen and ate their final meal of pot soup and crackers in silence.

"Well, that's that," he said as he finished.

"You know, we really don't need the clock any more. We only used it so we'd know when to eat."

He made no reply, so she continued.

"Allan, please, let's go outside now."

"No."

"We'll starve to death if we stay here."

"And we'll die of radiation if we don't. That's for damn sure. That fucking needle hasn't dropped below six thousand since the bomb."

"Maybe it's broken. I'd rather take my chances out there."

"Well, I wouldn't. Our chances are exactly zero up there."

"Maybe, but they're the same down here. If I have to die, I'd rather do it outside than in this tomb. We don't know what it's like up there; I want to see it. I know I'll die if I stay down here."

"And I know I'll die if we go upstairs."

"You don't have to go. Just let me go."

"The minute we open that hatch, this whole shelter will be contaminated."

"Please, Allan, please."

He rose. "You're getting hysterical," he said. "Shut up." When she didn't, he slapped her. "How many times do we have to go over this before it becomes clear to you that we're staying here?"

Allan emptied the bottle of cockroaches he had captured into the boiling water and cooked them till the bodies became soft and the water turned brown. Then he drained off the liquid and mashed the bodies into a pulp and seasoned it with pepper. He brought the pot and a large spoon to the table and sat across from Pam.

"See? They look just like refried beans."

"I just can't eat that," she replied slowly.

"So don't." He took a small mouthful and swallowed without chewing.

"It's not bad," he said after washing in down with a hearty drink of cold water. He took three more mouthfuls before he vomited. Pam watched him retching and looked away only once to glance furtively at the stairs. When he had finished, she stretched her hand out to him, but he stumbled to the sink to wash his face. She followed.

"Oh, Allan," she sighed, touching him. "Don't you see?"

128

"Shut up," he said and walked feebly to the bed where he flopped, face down and still.

Allan was trying to read, but he could scarcely keep his eyes or mind on the book. He looked around the room. Then at his book. And again around the room. Pam, familiar fixture, was missing.

Not wishing to disturb the stillness, or the faint sound he thought he heard, he rose and walked to the far end of the room. Looking up, he saw her carefully turning the wheel of the safety lock on the hatch.

Forgetting his weakened body, he bounded up the stairs two at a time, reaching her before she could finish. He grabbed her tightly around the neck and waist and pulled. As her clenched fingers slipped from the wheel, he jerked her free and flung her down the stairs. Then he re-tightened the lock.

He was still in a rage when he turned to walk down the stairs. He wanted to kill her, no, just beat the shit out of her for having nearly killed them both. He found her crumpled on the floor at the bottom of the stairs, her neck hideously twisted, and blood dripping from her nose and head.

He cradled her limp body in his arms, hugged her and carried her to the bed. There, he laid her gently on her back and tried to close her eyes, getting them only half-closed. He stroked her head slowly and kissed her lightly on the lips. The warm blood around her mouth had a pleasant flavor. Slowly, he kissed her face until it was clean.

When he lifted her to remove her blouse, there was a wet, red stain on the pillow where her head had been. With one hand, he held her upright; with the other, he slipped the blouse off her shoulders and, a bit awkwardly, pulled the sleeves off her arms. Carefully, he laid her back down in the same place, and smoothed the hair around her face. Leaning over, he rested his head on her chest, so still and warm and soft, as if nothing had changed. He reached for her breast and stuffed it in his mouth. He sucked it endlessly, harder and harder, and fondled it with his teeth. He chewed it harder and harder, but could not bring himself to chew hard enough to feed his body. Having lost her, he needed her, wanted her, loved her more than ever. His mouth hurt and he forgot about her breast. He noticed his hard-on.

He rose and unhurriedly began to remove his clothing. When he was naked, he looked at her again and reconfirmed his need. He unzipped her jeans, removed them methodically and spread her legs. She did not resist, but lay there passive and still as the first night, wanting him in her quiet way. Smooth, warm skin welcomed him and he entered easily.

He lay still for a while digging the feel of her closeness. Then he began to make soft, slow love to her, just the way she liked. As he moved, her body kept perfect time with his slow, steady rhythm. She followed exactly his every movement as he slowly increased the tempo. They moved together as they had never moved before. Together. He came forever.

And fell asleep.

When he awoke, later, her body was stiff and chilled beside him. Hard and really dead. He rolled out of bed and blindly heaped the bedclothes over it, obscuring it. He took a blanket and a pillow out of one of the cabinets and curled up on the floor in front of the toilet, where he stayed as his stomach shriveled in upon itself, dragging his other organs after it.

He slept and woke fitfully, sometimes noticing the pile of linen on the bed. But there was no food in the kitchen and no need to go to that end of the room. Daily, he felt less and less, either physically or emotionally, about his condition.

Eventually, he noticed a fetid odor. It persisted and demanded his attention. He decided to look at her body once more, just look at it. He knew it would look different—inhuman—a piece of meat. He still felt hunger.

When he drew back the covers for the first time in however long it had been, some of the cockroaches scurried off the bed, but others merely burrowed deeper into the decaying flesh, continuing their feast along the way. He covered it again and went back to his place on the floor and lay down.

An unmeasured moment of time passed before Mrs. Amis came to clean up. She had a devil of a time getting rid of the cockroaches and finally had to fumigate before she could run the ad again.

With her new tenants settling in, Mrs. Amis could relax once again. Propped up on pillows, under thick blankets in a massive four-poster, she watched the maid depart. And pouring herself a cup of tea, she reached for the remote control and switched on the monitor, leaned back and relaxed.

Foreword to Masks

Damon Knight, like many of the best of the older science fiction writers, is a talent of several parts, as if the demands of writing, editing, or criticism, taken by themselves, were simply not enough to contain his sensibility.

There have been pitifully few science fiction critics and of these none can match Knight for sophistication of insight, eye for technical detail, or usefulness to the development of writers. Damon Knight is virtually the only technical critic of science fiction worthy of the name. In recent years, the absence of his critical writing has been seriously felt.

Knight is also one of the best and most influential editors in the science fiction field. The ORBIT books, his quarterly anthologies of original speculative fiction, have introduced and developed more good new speculative writers than any other outlet for short speculative fiction in the English-speaking world, with the possible exception of *New Worlds*. Moreover, ORBIT was the very first of the "book-magazines" of original speculative fiction which are now the major American showcase for short speculative fiction and the development grounds of the best new writers. If there is a renaissance of short speculative fiction in process in the United States, Damon Knight must be considered the editor most responsible. Further, Knight is the originator and majordomo of the Milford Science Fiction Writers Conference, held annually in his spooky old Victorian manse. Here his talents as critic, editor, and writer merge. He was also a founder and first President of the Science Fiction Writers of America.

But in a very real sense, all this is incidental to Damon Knight, the writer. For reasons of his own, Knight has not written much fiction in the past few years; perhaps this is why some people tend to forget how far ahead of his time he was in the fifties and early sixties. Stories like "Rule Golden," "Stranger Station," and "The Handler" would stand out in the company of the very best contemporary speculative fiction. A decade ago, Knight was writing with a literary sophistication, artistic concern, and psychological depth that ten years later was to be considered revolutionary when it appeared in the work of younger science fiction writers.

It is difficult to determine why Knight's production of fiction fell off as it did. It is almost as if he stood back and waited for the field to catch up with the best of his work, while doing his best as an editor and critic to bring this transformation about. Perhaps he simply got so involved in creative editing that he didn't have the time to concentrate on fiction.

But whatever the reason, "Masks" is ample proof that Knight-the-writer is alive and well in Milford, Pennsylvania. He has taken a straightforward science fiction notion that other writers have toyed with before, and transformed it into a work of disturbing psychological depth and inner verisimilitude. Moreover, he has crafted the story so well that it appeared in *Playboy,* a magazine not noted for printing science fiction with this degree of depth or extrapolative vigor. He has not stepped outside the bounds of traditional science fiction here, rather he has written a story which satisfies its demands while transcending its limitations.

MASKS

by Damon Knight

The eight pens danced against the moving strip of paper, like the nervous claws of some mechanical lobster. Roberts, the technician, frowned over the tracings while the other two watched.

"Here's the wake-up impulse," he said, pointing with a skinny finger. "Then here, look, seventeen seconds more, still dreaming."

"Delayed response," said Babcock, the project director. His heavy face was flushed and he was sweating. "Nothing to worry about."

"OK, delayed response, but look at the difference in the tracings. Still dreaming, after the wake-up impulse, but the peaks are closer together. Not the same dream. More anxiety, more motor pulses."

"Why does he have to sleep at all?" asked Sinescu, the man from Washington. He was dark, narrow-faced. "You flush the fatigue poisons out, don't you? So what is it, something psychological?"

"He needs to dream," said Babcock. "It's true he has no physiological need for sleep, but he's got to dream. If

134

he didn't, he'd start to hallucinate, maybe go psychot-ic."

"Psychotic," said Sinescu. "Well—that's the question, isn't it? How long has he been doing this?"

"About six months."

"In other words, about the time he got his new body —and started wearing a mask?"

"About that. Look, let me tell you something: He's rational. Every test—"

"Yes, OK, I know about tests. Well—so he's awake now?"

The technician glanced at the monitor board. "He's up. Sam and Irma are with him." He hunched his shoulders, staring at the EEG tracings again. "I don't know why it should bother me. It stands to reason, if he has dream needs of his own that we're not satisfying with the programmed stuff, this is where he gets them in." His face hardened. "I don't know. Something about those peaks I don't like."

Sinescu raised his eyebrows. "You program his dreams?"

"Not program," said Babcock impatiently. "A routine suggestion to dream the sort of thing we tell him to. Somatic stuff, sex, exercise, sport."

"And whose idea was that?"

"Psych section. He was doing fine neurologically, every other way, but he was withdrawing. Psych decided he needed that somatic input in some form, we had to keep him in touch. He's alive, he's functioning, everything works. But don't forget, he spent forty-three years in a normal human body."

In the hush of the elevator, Sinescu said, "Washington."

Swaying, Babcock said, "I'm sorry; what?"

"You look a little rocky. Getting any sleep?"

"Not lately. What did you say before?"

"I said they're not happy with your reports in Washington."

"Goddamn it, I know that." The elevator door silently opened. A tiny foyer, green carpet, gray walls. There were three doors, one metal, two heavy glass. Cool, stale air. "This way."

Sinescu paused at the glass door, glanced through: a gray-carpeted living room, empty. "I don't see him."

"Around the el. Getting his morning checkup."

The door opened against slight pressure; a battery of ceiling lights went on as they entered. "Don't look up," said Babcock. "Ultraviolet." A faint hissing sound stopped when the door closed.

"And positive pressure in here? To keep out germs? Whose idea was that?"

"His." Babcock opened a chrome box on the wall and took out two surgical masks. "Here, put this on."

Voices came muffled from around the bend of the room. Sinescu looked with distaste at the white mask, then slowly put it over his head.

They stared at each other. "Germs," said Sinescu through the mask. "Is that rational?"

"All right, he can't catch a cold, or what have you, but think about it a minute. There are just two things now that could kill him. One is a prosthetic failure, and we guard against that; we've got five hundred people here, we check him out like an airplane. That leaves a cerebrospinal infection. Don't go in there with a closed mind."

The room was large, part living room, part library, part workshop. Here was a cluster of Swedish-modern chairs, a sofa, coffee table; here a workbench with a metal lathe, electric crucible, drill press, parts bins, tools on wallboards; here a drafting table; here a free-standing wall of bookshelves that Sinescu fingered curiously as they passed. Bound volumes of project reports, technical journals, reference books; no fiction, except for

Fire and Storm by George Stewart and *The Wizard of Oz* in a worn blue binding. Behind the bookshelves, set into a little alcove, was a glass door through which they glimpsed another living room, differently furnished: upholstered chairs, a tall philodendron in a ceramic pot. "There's Sam," Babcock said.

A man had appeared in the other room. He saw them, turned to call to someone they could not see, then came forward, smiling. He was bald and stocky, deeply tanned. Behind him, a small pretty woman hurried up. She crowded through after her husband, leaving the door open. Neither of them wore a mask.

"Sam and Irma have the next suite," Babcock said. "Company for him; he's got to have somebody around. Sam is an old Air Force buddy of his and, besides, he's got a tin arm."

The stocky man shook hands, grinning. His grip was firm and warm. "Want to guess which one?" He wore a flowered sport shirt. Both arms were brown, muscular and hairy; but when Sinescu looked more closely, he saw that the right one was a slightly different color, not quite authentic.

Embarrassed, he said, "The left, I guess."

"Nope." Grinning wider, the stocky man pulled back his right sleeve to show the straps.

"One of the spin-offs from the project," said Babcock. "Myoelectric, servo-controlled, weighs the same as the other one. Sam, they about through in there?"

"Maybe so. Let's take a peek. Honey, you think you could rustle up some coffee for the gentlemen?"

"Oh, why sure." The little woman turned and darted back through the open doorway.

The far wall was glass, covered by a translucent white curtain. They turned the corner. The next bay was full of medical and electronic equipment, some built into the walls, some in tall black cabinets on wheels. Four men in white coats were gathered around

137

what looked like an astronaut's couch. Sinescu could see someone lying on it: feet in Mexican woven-leather shoes, dark socks, gray slacks. A mutter of voices.

"Not through yet," Babcock said. "Must have found something else they didn't like. Let's go out onto the patio a minute."

"Thought they checked him at night—when they exchange his blood, and so on . . . ?"

"They do." Babcock said. "And in the morning, too." He turned and pushed open the heavy glass door. Outside, the roof was paved with cut stone, enclosed by a green-plastic canopy and tinted-glass walls. Here and there were concrete basins, empty. "Idea was to have a roof garden out here, something green, but he didn't want it. We had to take all the plants out, glass the whole thing in."

Sam pulled out metal chairs around a white table and they all sat down. "How is he, Sam?" asked Babcock.

He grinned and ducked his head. "Mean in the mornings."

"Talk to you much? Play any chess?"

"Not too much. Works, mostly. Reads some, watches the box a little." His smile was forced; his heavy fingers were clasped together and Sinescu saw now that the finger tips of one hand had turned darker, the others not. He looked away.

"You're from Washington, that right?" Sam asked politely. "First time here? Hold on." He was out of his chair. Vague upright shapes were passing behind the curtained glass door. "Looks like they're through. If you gentlemen would just wait here a minute, till I see." He strode across the roof. The two men sat in silence. Babcock had pulled down his surgical mask; Sinescu noticed and did the same.

"Sam's wife is a problem," Babcock said, leaning nearer. "It seemed like a good idea at the time, but she's lonely here, doesn't like it—no kids—"

The door opened again and Sam appeared. He had a mask on, but it was hanging under his chin. "If you gentlemen would come in now."

In the living area, the little woman, also with a mask hanging around her neck, was pouring coffee from a flowered ceramic jug. She was smiling brightly but looked unhappy. Opposite her sat someone tall, in gray shirt and slacks, leaning back, legs out, arms on the arms of his chair, motionless. Something was wrong with his face.

"Well, now," said Sam heartily. His wife looked up at him with an agonized smile.

The tall figure turned its head and Sinescu saw with an icy shock that its face was silver, a mask of metal with oblong slits for eyes, no nose or mouth, only curves that were faired into each other. "Project," said an inhuman voice.

Sinescu found himself half bent over a chair. He sat down. They were all looking at him. The voice resumed. "I said, are you here to pull the plug on the project?" It was unaccented, indifferent.

"Have some coffee." The woman pushed a cup toward him.

Sinescu reached for it, but his hand was trembling and he drew it back. "Just a fact-finding expedition," he said.

"Bull. Who sent you—Senator Hinkel?"

"That's right."

"Bull. He's been here himself; why send you? If you are going to pull the plug, might as well tell me." The face behind the mask did not move when he spoke, the voice did not seem to come from it.

"He's just looking around, Jim," said Babcock.

"Two hundred million a year," said the voice, "to keep one man alive. Doesn't make much sense, does it? Go on, drink your coffee."

Sinescu realized that Sam and his wife had already

139

finished theirs and that they had pulled up their masks. He reached for his cup hastily.

"Hundred percent disability in my grade is thirty thousand a year. I could get along on that easy. For almost an hour and a half."

"There's no intention of terminating the project," Sinescu said.

"Phasing it out, though. Would you say phasing it out?"

"Manners, Jim," said Babcock.

"OK. My worst fault. What do you want to know?"

Sinescu sipped his coffee. His hands were still trembling. "That mask you're wearing," he started.

"Not for discussion. No comment, no comment. Sorry about that; don't mean to be rude; a personal matter. Ask me something—" Without warning, he stood up, blaring, "Get that damn thing out of here!" Sam's wife's cup smashed, coffee brown across the table. A fawn-colored puppy was sitting in the middle of the carpet, cocking its head, brighteyed, tongue out.

The table tipped, Sam's wife struggled up behind it. Her face was pink, dripping with tears. She scooped up the puppy without pausing and ran out. "I better go with her," Sam said, getting up.

"Go on; and, Sam, take a holiday. Drive her into Winnemucca, see a movie."

"Yeah, guess I will." He disappeared behind the book-shelf wall.

The tall figure sat down again, moving like a man; it leaned back in the same posture, arms on the arms of the chair. It was still. The hands gripping the wood were shapely and perfect but unreal: there was something wrong about the fingernails. The brown, well-combed hair above the mask was a wig; the ears were wax. Sinescu nervously fumbled his surgical mask over his mouth and nose. "Might as well get along," he said, and stood up.

"That's right, I want to take you over to Engineering

and R and D," said Babcock. "Jim, I'll be back in a little while. Want to talk to you."

"Sure," said the motionless figure.

Babcock had had a shower, but sweat was soaking through the armpits of his shirt again. The silent elevator, the green carpet, a little blurred. The air cool, stale. Seven years, blood and money, 500 good men. Psych section, Cosmetic Engineering, R and D, Medical, Immunology, Supply, Serology, Administration. The glass doors. Sam's apartment empty, gone to Winnemucca with Irma. Psych. Good men, but were they the best? Three of the best had turned it down. Buried in the files. *Not like an ordinary amputation, this man has had everything cut off.*

The tall figure had not moved. Babcock sat down. The silver mask looked back at him.

"Jim, let's level with each other."

"Bad, huh?"

"Sure it's bad. I left him in his room with a bottle. I'll see him again before he leaves, but God knows what he'll say in Washington. Listen, do me a favor, take that thing off."

"Sure." The hand rose, plucked at the edge of the silver mask, lifted it away. Under it, the tan-pink face, sculptured nose and lips, eyebrows, eyelashes, not handsome but good-looking, normal-looking. Only the eyes wrong, pupils too big. And the lips that did not open or move when it spoke. "I can take anything off. What does that prove?"

"Jim, Cosmetic spent eight and a half months on that model and the first thing you do is slap a mask over it. We've asked you what's wrong, offered to make any changes you want."

"No comment."

"You talked about phasing out the project. Did you think you were kidding?"

141

A pause. "Not kidding."

"All right, then open up, Jim, tell me; I have to know. They won't shut the project down; they'll keep you alive, but that's all. There are seven hundred on the volunteer list, including two U.S. Senators. Suppose one of them gets pulled out of an auto wreck tomorrow. We can't wait till then to decide; we've got to know now. Whether to let the next one die or put him into a TP body like yours. So talk to me."

"Suppose I tell you something, but it isn't the truth."

"Why would you lie?"

"Why do you lie to a cancer patient?"

"I don't get it. Come on, Jim."

"OK, try this. Do I look like a man to you?"

"Sure."

"Bull. Look at this face." Calm and perfect. Beyond the fake irises, a wink of metal. "Suppose we had all the other problems solved and I could go into Winnemucca tomorrow; can you see me walking down the street— going into a bar—taking a taxi?"

"Is that all it is?" Babcock drew a deep breath. "Jim, sure there's a difference, but for Christ's sake, it's like any other prosthesis—people get used to it. Like that arm of Sam's. You see it, but after a while you forget it, you don't notice."

"Bull. You pretend not to notice. Because it would embarrass the cripple."

Babcock looked down at his clasped hands. "Sorry for yourself?"

"Don't give me that," the voice blared. The tall figure was standing. The hands slowly came up, the fists clenched. "I'm in this thing. I've been in it for two years. I'm in it when I go to sleep, and when I wake up, I'm still in it."

Babcock looked up at him. "What do you want, facial mobility? Give us twenty years, maybe ten, we'll lick it."

"I want you to close down Cosmetic."

142

"But that's—"

"Just listen. The first model looked like a tailor's dummy, so you spent eight months and came up with this one, and it looks like a corpse. The whole idea was to make me look like a man, the first model pretty good, the second model better, until you've got something that can smoke cigars and joke with women and go bowling and nobody will know the difference. You can't do it, and if you could what for?"

"I don't—Let me think about this. What do you mean, a metal—"

"Metal, sure, but what difference does that make? I'm talking about shape, Function. Wait a minute." The tall figure strode across the room, unlocked a cabinet, came back with rolled sheets of paper. "Look at this."

The drawing showed an oblong metal box on four jointed legs. From one end protruded a tiny mushroom-shaped head on a jointed stem and a cluster of arms ending in probes, drills, grapples. "For moon prospecting."

"Too many limbs," said Babcock after a moment. "How would you—"

"With the facial nerves. Plenty of them left over. Or here." Another drawing. "A module plugged into the control system of a spaceship. That's where I belong, in space. Sterile environment, low grav, I can go where a man can't go and do what a man can't do. I can be an asset, not a Goddamn billion-dollar liability."

Babcock rubbed his eyes. "Why didn't you say anything before?"

"You were all hipped on prosthetics. You would have told me to tend my knitting."

Babcock's hands were shaking as he rolled up the drawings. "Well, by God, this just may do it. It just might." He stood up and turned toward the door. "Keep your—" He cleared his throat. "I mean, hang tight, Jim."

"I'll do that."

When he was alone, he put on his mask again and stood motionless a moment, eye shutters closed. Inside, he was running clean and cool; he could feel the faint reassuring hum of pumps, click of valves and relays. They had given him that: cleaned out all the offal, replaced it with machinery that did not bleed, ooze or suppurate. He thought of the lie he had told Babcock. *Why do you lie to a cancer patient?* But they would never get it, never understand.

He sat down at the drafting table, clipped a sheet of paper to it and with a pencil began to sketch a rendering of the moon-prospector design. When he had blocked in the prospector itself, he began to draw the background of craters. His pencil moved more slowly and stopped; he put it down with a click.

No more adrenal glands to pump adrenaline into his blood, so he could not feel fright or rage. They had released him from all that—love, hate, the whole sloppy mess—but they had forgotten there was still one emotion he could feel.

Sinescu, with the black bristles of his beard sprouting through his oily skin. A whitehead ripe in the crease beside his nostrils.

Moon landscape, clean and cold. He picked up the pencil again.

Babcock, with his broad pink nose shining with grease, crusts of white matter in the corners of his eyes. Food mortar between his teeth.

Sam's wife, with raspberry-colored paste on her mouth. Face smeared with tears, a bright bubble in one nostril. And the damn dog, shiny nose, wet eyes . . .

He turned. The dog was there, sitting on the carpet, wet red tongue out *left the door open again* dripping, wagged its tail twice, then started to get up. He reached for the metal T square, leaned back, swinging it like an ax, and the dog yelped once as metal sheared bone, one eye spouting red, writhing on its back, dark stain of piss across the carpet and he hit it again, hit it again

The body lay twisted on the carpet, fouled with blood, ragged black lips drawn back from teeth. He wiped off the T square with a paper towel, then scrubbed it in the sink with soap and steel wool, dried it and hung it up. He got a sheet of drafting paper, laid it on the floor, rolled the body over onto it without spilling any blood on the carpet. He lifted the body in the paper, carried it out onto the patio, then onto the unroofed section, opening the doors with his shoulder. He looked over the wall. Two stories down, concrete roof, vents sticking out of it, nobody watching. He held the dog out, let it slide off the paper, twisting as it fell. It struck one of the vents, bounced, a red smear. He carried the paper back inside, poured the blood down the drain, then put the paper into the incinerator chute.

Splashes of blood were on the carpet, the feet of the drafting table, the cabinet, his trouser legs. He sponged them all up with paper towels and warm water. He took off his clothing, examined it minutely, scrubbed it in the sink, then put it in the washer. He washed the sink, rubbed himself down with disinfectant and dressed again. He walked through into Sam's silent apartment, closing the glass door behind him. Past the potted philodendron, over-stuffed furniture, red-and-yellow painting on the wall, out onto the roof, leaving the door ajar. Then back through the patio, closing doors.

Too bad. How about some goldfish.

He sat down at the drafting table. He was running clean and cool. The dream this morning came back to his mind, the last one, as he was struggling up out of sleep: *slithery kidneys burst gray lungs blood and hair ropes of guts covered with yellow fat oozing and sliding and oh god the stink like the breath of an outhouse no sound nowhere he was putting a yellow stream down the slide of the dunghole and*

He began to ink in the drawing, first with a fine steel pen, then with a nylon brush. *his heel slid and he was falling could not stop himself, falling into slimy bulging softness higher than his chin, higher and he could not move paralyzed and he tried to scream tried to scream tried to scream*

The prospector was climbing a crater slope with its handling members retracted and its head tilted up. Behind it the distant ringwall and the horizon, the black sky, the pinpoint stars. And he was there, and it was not far enough, not yet, for the earth hung overhead like a rotten fruit, blue with mold, crawling, wrinkling, purulent and alive.

Foreword to PENNIES, OFF A DEAD MAN'S EYES

Perhaps the man most closely associated with the phrase New Wave in American speculative fiction is Harlan Ellison. His huge anthology of original stories, *Dangerous Visions,* was perhaps the single most important book of short science fiction published in the sixties. Thirty-two writers were told to write anything they wanted to, that the conventions of the genre were lifted, especially with regard to controversial content. At least a dozen of the stories in that book represented landmarks of one sort of another for the writers involved. Curiously, some of the most significant gains made by writers involved in that book were in the area of style rather than content, an indication that restrictions in one aspect of writing tend to produce restricted thinking in general.

Ellison himself, as a writer, successfully made the transition from the old traditions of commercial science fiction to the new speculative fiction of the mid-sixties and seventies. In the earlier stages of his career, he wrote large amounts of commercial science fiction for the pulp magazines, much of it of little outstanding literary merit. But even in the early stages of his career, he stood apart from the typical science fiction writer in the breadth of his scope. Not only did he write science fiction successfully, he was publishing mainstream fiction, film, literary, and music criticism, nonfiction, and even autobiography. He was never a science fiction writer, but always a writer who wrote science fiction.

His fiction seems to have come into full flower about the time he began to write films and television. As with Robert Silverberg, whose career parallels his in certain ways, Ellison's true literary love had always been science fiction; when his screen writing career removed the economic impetus for writing genre science fiction,

Ellison gradually began to channel the diverse elements of his total output of fiction into a synthesized style and range of content uniquely his own, but unquestionably speculative fiction.

"Pennies, Off a Dead Man's Eyes" is a good example of some of the qualities of Ellison's later short stories. The story is unquestionably speculative fiction, yet the speculative element stands to one side of the story's main thrust, never dominating it. On the other hand, the speculative element isn't simply thrown in to qualify the story as "science fiction"; it is an integral part of the story, albeit a minor part. This treatment of speculative elements is common in Ellison's later work. His main concern is character and human relationships—and sometimes theology—and the degree of importance of the speculative element in a given story is determined by the use it can be put to in dealing with these primary concerns. Ellison's later work is clearly that of one who writes speculative fiction by story-to-story choice, a writer perfectly at home in "mainstream" fiction, rather than one who must lean on speculative elements as a creative or commercial crutch.

In this respect, Ellison now stands clearly on the modern side of the divide in speculative fiction, though he began his career as a commercial science fiction writer. Like Silverberg, he has made the transition from commercially defined science fiction to personally impelled creation of idiosyncratic speculative fiction.

PENNIES, OFF A DEAD MAN'S EYES

by Harlan Ellison

It was a slow freight in from Kansas City. I'd nearly emptied all the fluid from my gut sac. There were no weeds or water to fill it again. When the freight hit the outermost switching lines of the yards it was already dark. I rolled myself off the edge of the boxcar, hit running, went twenty feet fast and slipped, fell to my hands and knees, and tumbled over. When I got up there were tiny bits of white chalk stone imbedded in my palms; I rubbed them off, but they really hurt.

I looked around, tried to gauge my position in relation to the town, and when I recognized the spire of the First Baptist, set off across the tracks in the right direction. There was a yard bull running like crazy toward me, so I went dark and left him standing where I'd been, scratching the back of his head and looking around.

It took me forty minutes to walk into the center of town, through it, and out the other side, in the direction of Littletown—the nigger section.

There was a coal bin entrance to the All-Holiness

Pentecostal Church of Christ the Master, and I slipped inside, smiling. In twelve years they hadn't repaired the latch and lock. The stairs were dim in the basement darkness, but I knew my way the way a child remembers his bedroom when the light is out. Across twelve years, I remembered.

There were the occasional dim rumblings of voices from upstairs, from the vestry, from the casket room, from the foyer.

Jedediah Parkman was laid out up there. Eighty-two years old, dead, tired, at the end of an endless road down which he had stumbled, black, poor, proud, helpless. No, not helpless.

I climbed the stairs from the basement, laid my white hand against the dry, cracked wood of the door, and thought of all the weight of black pressing back on the other side. Jed would have chuckled.

Through a crack in the jamb I saw nothing but wall opposite; I carefully opened the door. The hall was empty. They'd be moving into the vestry now. The service would be beginning. The preacher would be getting ready to tell the congregation about old Jed, what a good man he'd been, how he always had enough heart for the stray cats and deadbeat kids he picked up. How so many people owed him so much. Jed would have snorted.

But I'd arrived in time. How many other stray cats had made it?

I closed the basement door behind me, slid along the wall to the pantry door that opened into the small room adjacent to the vestry. In a moment I was inside. I turned off the light in the pantry, in case I had to go dark, then I crept to the door in the opposite wall. I opened it a sliver and peered out into the vestry.

Since the bombing the chapel had been unusable. I'd heard about it even in Chicago: seven had been killed, and Deacon Wilkie'd been blinded by flying glass. They'd made do the best they could with the vestry.

Folding chairs were set up in rows. They were filled with the population of Littletown. They were two deep around the walls. One or two white faces. I recognized a couple of other stray cats. It'd been twelve years: they looked as though they were making it. But they hadn't forgotten.

I watched, and counted blacks. One hundred and eighteen. A few days ago, I'd been in Kansas City, there'd been one hundred and nineteen. Now the one hundred and nineteenth black man in Danville's Littletown lay in his casket, atop sawhorses, in the front of the room, surrounded by flowers.

Hello, old Jed.

Twelve, it's been.

God, you're quiet. No chuckles, no laughs, Jed. You're dead. I know.

He lay, hands folded across his chest. Big catcher's mitt paws folded, calluses hidden—sweet Jesus, I could see flickering candle light glinting off his nails. *They'd manicured his hands!* Old Jed would've screamed, doing a thing like that to a man bit his nails to the quick!

Laying up in a shallow box, neat black patent leather shoes pointing toward the ceiling; kinky salt-and-pepper hair flattened against the silk lining of the box (eighty-two, and that old man's hair still had black in it!); lay in his best suit, a black suit, clean white long-sleeve shirt and a yellow tie. On display. Looking down at himself, for sure, from the Heaven he'd always believed was up there. Looking down at himself so fine, and smiling; puffing proud, yes *sir!*

On each of his eyes, a silver dollar.

To pay his way with the Man, across the River Jordan.

I didn't go in. Never intended to. Too many questions. Some of them might've remembered; I know the other stray cats would've. So I just laid back, and waited to talk to old Jed private.

The service was a brief one, they cried a decent amount. Then it was over and they filed past slowly. A couple of women did the big falling down trying to get in the box thing with him. Christ knows what Jed would've done with *that*. I waited till the room emptied out. Preacher and a couple of the brothers cleaned up, decided to leave the chairs till morning, shut off the lights, and went. There was silence and a lot of shadows, just the candles still doing their slow motion. I waited a long time, just to make sure, then finally I opened the door a bit more and started to step through.

There was a sound from the door to the outside, and I pulled back fast. I watched as the door opened and a tall, slim woman in black came down among the chairs toward the open casket. Veil over her face.

My gut sac went total empty right then. Lining started to burn. I thought sure she'd heard the rumbling. Sprayed it with stomach juice and that would hold it for a while till I could get weed and water. Burned.

I couldn't make out her face behind the veil. She walked up to the casket and stared down at Jed Parkman. Then she reached out a gloved hand toward the body, pulled it back, tried again and then held the hand motionless in the air above the cold meat. Slowly she swept the veil back over the wide-brimmed hat.

I drew in a breath. She was a white woman. More than just ordinarily beautiful. Stunning. One of those creatures God made just to be looked at. I held my breath; breathing would release the sound of the blood in my temples, scare her away.

She kept looking at the corpse, then slowly she reached out again. Carefully, very carefully, she removed the coins from Jed's dead eyes. She dropped them in her purse. Then she dropped the veil, and started to turn away. She stopped, turned back, kissed her fingertips and touched the cold lips of the penniless dead one.

Then she turned around and left the vestry. Very quickly.

I stood unmoving, watching nothing, chill and lost.

When you take the money off a dead man's eyes, it means he can't pay his passage to Heaven.

That white woman sent Jedediah Parkman straight to Hell.

I went after her.

If I hadn't keeled over, I'd have caught her before she got on the train.

She wasn't far ahead of me, but my gut was burning so bad, I knew if I didn't get some grass or weeds in it, I'd be in wicked shape. That happened once in Seattle. I barely got out of the emergency ward before they could X-ray me. Broke into the hospital kitchen, pumped about eight pounds of Caesar salad and half a bottle of Sparkletts water into my sac and wound up bareass cold in a hospital gown, out on a Seattle street in the dead of winter.

Hadn't thought that for a second before I went over on my face, half a block from the Danville train station. Legs went idiot on me and over I go. Had just enough sense to go dark before I hit. Lay there, a car might run me over. No idea how long I was out, but not long. Came back and crawled on my belly like a reptile onto a patch of grass. Chewed, pulling myself on my elbows. Got enough in to get myself up, staggered the half block to the station, fell onto the water fountain stuck on the wall. Drank till the stationmaster leaned way over the ticket window, staring. Couldn't go dark, he'd seen me.

"You got business here, mister?"

I felt the lava juices subsiding. I could walk. Went up to him, said, "My fiancée, you know, a bad fight, she come down this way . . . ." I let it wait. He watched me, wasn't giving away a little thing free.

"Look, we're supposed to be married next Thursday

153

—I'm sorry I yelled at her. Half out of my, well, hell, mister, have you seen her? Tall girl, all in black, wearing a veil?" Sounded like a description of Mata Hari.

Old man scratched at the beard he'd sprouted since he'd come on at noon. "She bought a ticket for KayCee. Train's 'bout to pull out."

Then I realized I'd been hearing the whoofing sounds of the train all this time. When my sac goes, everything goes. I started hearing and smelling and feeling the grain of the ticket counter under my hands. And bolted out the door. Train was just getting ready to slide; express freight was almost loaded. Behind me, the stationmaster was bellowing. "Ticket! Hey, mister . . . ticket!"

"Get it by the conductor!" And I vaulted up onto the coach platform. The train edged out.

I pushed open the door to the coach and looked down the rows of pullman seats. She was there, looking out the window into the darkness. I started toward her, but thought better of it. There were a couple of dozen passengers between her and me. I couldn't do anything here, now, anyway. I dropped into a scungy seat, and puffs of dust went into the air.

I slid down and took off my right shoe. The twenty was folded neat against the instep. It was all I'd put aside. But I knew the conductor would be along to punch my ticket. And I didn't want to get caught like Jed Parkman. I wanted my fare to be paid.

We'd see about it in Kansas City.

It was a change. Riding inside.

She went to a phone booth and dialed a place without looking up the number. I waited. She went out to stand in front of the terminal. After a while a car with two women came up, and she got in. I went dark and opened the back door and slid in. They looked around and didn't see anything in the shadows back there, and the heavyset woman driving said, "Now what the hell was *that?*" and the pimply one with the plastic hair, the one in the middle, reached over the seat back and thumbed down the lock.

"Wind," she said.

"What wind?" the truck said. But she pulled out.

I always liked K.C. Nice ride. Even in winter. But I didn't like the women. Not one of them.

They drove out, almost to the Missouri border, toward Weston. I knew a bourbon distillery out there. Best ever made. The truck pulled in at a big house set apart from slummy-looking places on a street with only one corner light. Whore house. Had to be. It was.

I didn't understand, but I'd by God certainly find out soon. I'd arrived, but Jed was still traveling.

The truck said, "You pay the girl."

I picked out the tall, slim one in the harem pants and halter top. She couldn't be smart, I thought. With a face like that, to wind down in a crib was some kind of special stupid. Or something else.

We went upstairs. The room was like any bedroom. There were stuffed animals on the bed, a giraffe with pink day-glo spots, a koala, floppy gopher or muskrat, I can't tell them apart. She had a photo of a movie star stuck in the frame of the bureau mirror. She took off the harem pants and I said, "We'll talk." She gave me a look I knew. Another freako. "That's two bucks extra," she said. I shook my heard. "Five should cover everything."

She shrugged, and sat down on the edge of the bed, her thin legs straight out in front of her.

We stared at each other.

"Why'd you send Jed to Hell?"

Her head snapped up on her neck, and she quivered like a hound on scent. She didn't even know how to ask me.

"You get the hell out of here!"

155

"I've got five bucks worth of something coming."

She bounced up off that bed, and went straight across the room. She was screaming before the door was open:

"Bren! Bren! C'mon, Bren! Help up here!"

I heard the foundations of the house shake and the rumble of artillery on the next hill, and then something big and hairy came at me. He had to come through the door sidewise. I put up my hands and that was all. He carried me straight across the room, into the bureau. My back snapped against the edge of the bureau and he bent me till everything started to slip up toward the ceiling. The girl ran out, still shouting. When she was gone I ended it for him.

There was a trellis outside the window. I went down until the ivy ripped loose, and I fell the rest of the way.

That night I slept on the front porch of the house next door, in the glider, watching the ambulance and then the police cars come and go. There were two unmarked police cars that stayed very late. I don't think they were on duty.

I waited two days, sleeping on the front porch of the house next door. I'd have gone dark more than I did, but there were three empty lots between me and the whore house, and the people with the front porch had gone away for a while. I suppose on a winter vacation, maybe. There was plenty of weed and grass around, and I let snow melt in an empty milk bottle. At night I'd go dark and steal Hydrox Cookies and milk and beef jerky from a twenty-four-hour market. I don't eat much, usually. Missed coffee, though.

On the second day I jimmied a window in the empty house. Just to be ready.

Toward evening of the second day, she came out.

I went dark, waited on the sidewalk for her, and she walked straight into my fist.

In the empty house, I laid her out on a canopied bed

in the master bedroom. When she came to and sat up, I was slouched in a chair across from the bed. She shook her head, looked around, focused, saw me, and started to let go with the screaming again. I sat forward in the chair and said, very softly, "Bren, what happened to him, I can do that again," and she looked sick, and shut her mouth. "Now we go back to where we were," I said, getting up. I walked over and stood there near her. She lay back, terrified, no other word for it.

"How did you know Jed?" My voice was level, but I was hurting.

"I'm his daughter."

"I can make you tell the truth."

"I'm not lying, I'm his . . . I was his daughter."

"You're white."

She didn't say anything.

"Okay, why did you send him to Hell? You know what it means to take the money."

She snorted a very shitty laugh.

"Lady, you better understand something. I don't know who the hell you are, but that old man found me when I was seven years old and kept me alive till I was old enough to go it on my own. Now he meant stuff to me, lady, so I can see myself getting mad enough at you to do just about *anything*. More green than even Bren. So you feel like telling me why you'd do something like that to a man who was kind to everybody?"

Her face went very hard. Even scared, she hated. "And just what the hell do *you* know? Yeah, he had kind for everybody. Everybody 'cept his own." Then, softly, "Everybody 'cept me."

I couldn't tell if she was sick, or deluded, or just putting me on. Lying? Not where she was. No reason for it. And she'd seen that Bren. No, she was telling the truth —if she believed it.

A white girl with old Jed for a father?

It didn't make any sense.

Unless . . .

There are some you can meet—the strange, twisted ones—and you know them by an aura, a scent, a *feel* about them, that if you had one *single word*—like "junkie" or "nympho" or "hooker" or "Bircher"—a key word that labeled their secret thing, you would understand all the inexplicable, off-center things about them. The one word people. One word and you've got the handle on them. One word like wino, or diabetic, or puritan, or—

"Passing."

She didn't answer. She just stared at me, and hated me. And I looked in her face to see it, now that I knew what it was, but it wasn't there, of course. She was good at it. And that explained what had been between her and old Jedediah Parkman. Why she'd kissed the dead meat and sent it straight to Hell. But not the kind of Hell Jed had consigned her to. If he'd had all that kind of love for stray cats like me, I could imagine how strong his hate and frustration and shame would have been at one of his own pretending to be what she wasn't.

"You never know about people," I said to her. "He took in all kinds, and didn't care where they came from, or what they were. Just as long as they didn't lie about it. He had a lot of love."

She was waiting for me to do something bad to her, what she thought she had coming. I laughed, but not the way Jed used to laugh. "Lady, I ain't your daddy. He's punished you all he's ever going to. And you and me, neither one of us is white, and we're too much alike for *me* to punish you."

Passing. How about that. She didn't know what the color line even *looked* like. Black for white: hell, that's a cinch. Jed, Jed, you poor old nigger bastard. You knew I couldn't get home again, and you taught me how to pass so they wouldn't kill me, but you couldn't handle it when it happened to you.

I pulled my last five bucks out of my pocket and

tossed it on the end of the bed. "Here, baby, get it changed and keep a couple of silver dollars for your own party. Maybe Jed'll be waiting and you can straighten it out between you."

Then I went dark and started to leave. She was staring at where I'd been, her mouth open, as I paused in the doorway. "And keep the change," I said.

After all, she'd paid the dues for me, hadn't she?

Foreword to 198–, A TALE OF "TOMORROW"

John T. Sladek, an American living in London, is probably one of the half-dozen most interesting and original writers of short speculative fiction in the English language, though little of even his best work has been published in the United States.

Sladek is fascinated, even obsessed, by programmed fiction. He has carried William Burroughs' ideas of randomly cut-up fiction one or two very important steps further. Where Burroughs took bits and pieces cut from various sources more or less randomly and put them together in semi-random fashion, Sladek writes his own "bits" and then constructs programs of varying complexity according to which he assembles the bits into stories, allowing a certain amount of randomness to enter the process as a "collaborator."

From another writer, such artificially constructed pieces might well emerge tendentious, dull, and unreadable; indeed several other writers have attempted this kind of thing with sterile results. But Sladek, even in his more conventional novels and stories, is a humorist, and his experimental pieces are first of all *funny*. There is no solemnity at all in them; it's obvious that Sladek had fun writing them, and the reader has fun reading them. In this respect, his experiments must be deemed successful: they evoke pleasurable responses in the reader.

I do not know precisely how "198–, A Tale of 'Tomorrow'" was written. Perhaps it is a programmed story, perhaps not. It does, however, read like Sladek's programmed pieces. If it was written in a more straightforward manner, then Sladek has somehow managed to learn how to build his "random-programmed" effects into entirely controlled and self-conscious writing, Zen speculative fiction, as it were. At this, the mind boggles, almost as it does at the thought of one of Sladek's pet ambitions: to collaborate on a novel with a computer.

198-, A TALE OF "TOMORROW"

by John T. Sladek

Ernest thought it would be fun to let his computer call up Frank's computer on the telephone.

"Good to hear yours, too! But hey, do you know what A.M. it is out here?"

Al is seen glancing at his watch. Thanks to a vibrating quartz crystal in it, this watch keeps very, very accurate time. He looks from its Swiss face to the American face of Dot, his wife, out in the backyard eating a piece of fruit that has been picked the day before yesterday in the Orient. Will miracles—or anything—ever cease? The digital clock reports a new minute.

"I met you," Al said into a portable tape recorder no larger than a package of cigarettes, "a year, three days, seven hours and forty-three minutes ago, through that computer dating service. You had brushed your teeth electrically, using stannous fluoride toothpaste to prevent decay. I had just had dacron veins put in.

"Times change. You now have someone else's liver and kidney; I have ridden on an atomic submarine."

On the atomic ship, Al will notice an interesting article about LSD, a drug commonly supposed to cause visions and insights. He would reproduce this article by xerography, a fast electrostatic process making use of powdered ink.

Al called Bertha, his ex-wife, on the hall video phone.

"I just took a stay-awake pill," she said. "I've been so sleepy ever since the sauna I took, on the airbus from———."

"What's new?"

"I'm pregnant again, due to the fertility drug I'm taking. Ah, and I have a new non-stick milk saucepan. See?" On the screen she cuts open a tetrahedral carton of milk which was sealed for almost a year, then pours some into a special pan. The pan has previously been coated with a compound to prevent sticking and burning. So Bertha, wife of Ernest, was pregnant!

She and Al soon fell into their old argument about riot control. She favored tanks with aluminium armor, while Al defended the judicious use of Mace, a gas which irritates the mucous membranes.

"What's new with you and Dot?" she asks.

"Oh, I've been sterilized. Dot has this detached retina, but luckily they can now weld it back on with lasers."

They spoke of Dot's trip to the Orient, on a ballistic, supersonic plane. There Dot makes the acquaintance of an amateur biologist named Frank, who's all keyed up about the isolation of the gene. His real business is the manufacture of cosmetics for men, in factories he claimed were 97 percent automated.

LIFE AFTER DEATH?—AL WONDERS

Ernest took a tranquilizer before he called Dot on the teletypewriter. They were lovers, not to Al's knowledge. This was a conveniently private mode of communication, not often used by spirit mediums, though.

As they "spoke," Ernest drank coffee that had been percolated, frozen, vacuum dried and packed in jars. A spoonful of this substance to a cup of boiling water, while Dot watched the five-inch screen of her portable television set; there is a baseball game in far-off Texas, played on nylon grass beneath a geodesic dome, and she is part of it. When they have said the private things lovers must, Dot took a sleeping pill and slept.

Clement, or Clem, was Al's son by a previous marriage. Next day he fuelled his car at a coin gas station, dry-cleaned his clothes in a similar manner, and fell foul of a peculiar police arrangement: At one end of a bridge police read the license numbers of all passing cars into their radios. The computer at headquarters checks these for old violations.

Clem lived avoiding the army in a module apartment house, which has been made up at a factory in complete, decorated rooms, then bolted together at the building site. When he gets home he tries to call Bertha, his former stepmother, by means of a telephone message relayed through a communications satellite many thousands of miles, but she is at the hospital, having her third child.

Bertha's first child was now a bright little five-year-old, using an unusual teaching machine to learn to type and spell at the same time. This machine would give an instruction, then lock all but the necessary keys. If only life could be like that, Al thought, with no chance to err! In a programmed novel, the reader determines the ending.

Her second child was very intelligent, possibly because Bertha wore a suit pressurized with oxygen during the brain-growing months of pregnancy. Her present delivery is difficult. The child has worked down too far for a Caesarian yet not far enough for forceps. What is the obstetrician to do?

He used a new suction device to grip the child's head and draw him from the womb. Soon it cried, and before long, Bertha knew, it would be joining its siblings in immunity to polio, once a dread crippler and killer of children. She only hoped it would grow up to be a president like the one she now watches on color TV, announcing the landing of men on the moon (this president had not yet been assassinated). O Frank, Frank! Where are you?

Frank had given up smoking, drinking and excessive eating since his heart-lung transplant. Yet here he is, enjoying a cigar, a martini, and what looks like beef Stroganoff! What can possibly be the explanation of this?

It was a photograph of Frank made many years before, to demonstrate a process that made color prints, right in the camera, seconds after the photo was snapped. Dot became a secretary. As she rode the helicopter to the Pan Am building, she typed on her personal portable plastic typewriter. The ride compared favorably with her former trip on the 125 mph train from Tokyo to Osaka, where she met Frank. Unforgettable Japan! She revisited in memory that factory where thousands of workers began the day with the company song, followed by "Zen jerks" to limber up mind and body for the assembly of portable record players.

Such as the one Clem now listened to as he avoided the draft. He did not want to die in Vietnam, but stay here, taking LSD. He saw God, was God, felt God, left God.

Frank was at this moment crossing the English Channel on a hovercraft. He liked unusual means of motion: In Paris he had stood upon a moving sidewalk. In London, he meant to ride on one of the famous "driverless" Underground trains. Back in the U.S., he tries sitting on the beetle-like back of his robot lawnmower, as it mows its random pattern. Travel was his vice. Like Ernest's drinking.

Ernest had thank God been cured of his drinking by aversion therapy. One by one, all the pleasant stimulus-response mechanisms linking him with alcohol were broken down. In real time, Al ponders life after death.

He had engaged a firm to freeze him soon after death and thus maintain him until such time as science should come across a way of reversing whatever killed him. Ernest would live longer than otherwise on account of his "pacemaker," an electronic device to regulate the heartbeat of Ernest. In a programmed novel, he might or might not have this pacemaker; it all depends on the reader.

Al dialed Ernest's number in another city. "Dialed" is not strictly accurate, for the clumsy dial on Al's phone had been replaced by pushbuttons and musical tones. They get into a heated discussion of missile defence systems. Ernest certainly presents his case fairly, but Al wouldn't listen to reason. Dot counted her contraceptive pills, twenty of which must be taken each month. She also changed her paper panties. Clem receives a picture of Frank by almost magical means!

Bertha puts the picture into a machine and places the receiver of her phone upon it. Far away, Clem copies this motion, then finds the picture in his duplicate machine. Eagerly, he gazes on the familiar lineaments of his real father.

Dot notices how much plastic there is around: Her plastic necklace, her boss's plastic tie, Al's plastic credit cards, which he claimed were displacing money in the realtime world—could there be any connection with that island where they issued bright plastic coins? Dot saw what she must do, later. Now—

She maintains that the "golfball" typewriter, a high-speed machine using interchangeable spherical type fonts, is a pain in the ass. The reader, Al, may choose . . .

Bertha took a new antibiotic tablet, while Ernest explained again the difference between "Quasars" and "Quarks":

" 'Quarks' are mathematical entities proposed to explain certain behavior in subatomic particles. 'Quasars' are quasi-stellar radio sources which have often puzzled astronomers." Clem tore Frank's picture into thirty-two pieces. Why can't the others share time, the whatyou-callems, the computer makers, the peoples? On a radio small as a pocket watch, Clem heard the news:

They had invented a polymer of water which, if un-controlled, could turn all the water of the world into plastic.

Dot and Frank are in bed when Al

No, Dot is at home, Al dies of heart failure in his of-fice, slumping across the digital calendar. "A black and white picture!" muttered Clem, as his heart begins to beat. "What do they take me for?" Dot and Ernest are in the vibrating bed. Clem hears of a plan to widen the Panama canal with atomic blasts. Dot and Ernest are vibrating when Al walks in with the electric carving knife in his hand. This carving knife could run as now on batteries. Alternatively, it could use house power, ul-timately derived from a distant atomic pile.

Foreword to FLIGHT USELESS, INEXORABLE THE PURSUIT

Thomas M. Disch is a writer of delicate grossness, or gross delicacy, if you prefer. His prose is perhaps the most precisely honed weapon in speculative fiction; this may have something to do with the fact that he is also a poet of some repute. His sense of irony is exquisite and never far away from the surface of what he is doing. Yet his prose reads simply and clearly and is never dense. He is arch only when archness is the effect he is trying to achieve. He walks a number of fine lines simultaneously in his fiction; he rarely stumbles and never falls.

Yet much of his material could hardly be called subtle, delicate, or abstruse. His best novel, *Camp Concentration,* is told from the first-person viewpoint of a slightly pretentious poet, but concerns itself with a variant of syphilis which produces spurts of genius on its way toward paresis and death and contains probably one of the most original notions of the end-of-the-world calamity in speculative fiction. Disch has an active and frequently nasty sense of humor. However, he is not primarily a humorous writer; most of his work is in deadly earnest. Humor, largely in the form of black irony, lurks beneath the surface of much of his serious work like some all-knowing but tolerant troll. Rather than sapping the power of his fiction, this undercurrent strengthens it and, paradoxically, makes it feel slightly sinister. The grin is sardonic, and in the irony lurk unpleasant truths that we recognize but would rather not have spoken aloud. There is something of the wolf in pussycat's clothing in Disch, and the mask has a way of slipping at strategic moments.

Disch can also turn things around and write overtly funny pieces with an existential bite at the end. In fact a

167

good deal of his work exists squarely on the fine line between "serious" fiction with ironically humorous undertones and "humorous" fiction with a scorpion's tail. Disch's work is filled and empowered with these sorts of carefully calculated tensions.

"Flight Useless, Inexorable the Pursuit," is a nice little example of Disch's delicacy of touch working against a certain grossness of subject, of his ability to create an involving mood, working against his sense of humor, the various tensions creating an esthetic whole that sits there vibrating in dynamic equilibrium.

FLIGHT USELESS, INEXORABLE

THE PURSUIT

by Thomas M. Disch

As he stumbled against the hedge, a car passed, brushing his face with its cruel light. The hedge trembled all along its length, like a large molded gelatin, and for minutes after the rimed and sickly leaves quivered. Thighs quivered. He ought not to run, but his terror . . . Consciously, he walked down the street of identical Tudor houses. 48, 46, 44, 42, 40, 38, never skipping a beat. Before some of the houses, the dozen or so square yards of lawn had been stripped away and replaced with asphalt or concrete. They had become miniature parking lots. The cold air performed surgeries in his lungs. He had lost his gloves, or forgotten them when he'd left the house. How long ago? The thing had caught sight of him returning from the bakery. The bag of jelly doughnuts was probably still where he had set it down, on the dinette table, growing stale. At seven, or maybe eight P.M. Now it was dark again. A night and a day gone by. Thinking of the doughnuts, he grew hungry though it was a false hunger: he had eaten several times during the day—sandwiches from delicatessens, teas and pastries at Lyons shops, sixpenny bags of crisps. Until his money had run out. He ought to have taken a train out of London at the start. Instead he'd squandered his money shuttling about town. Always when he stopped —in Stepney, in Bethnal Green, in Camden Town, it found him out. How did it track him? How had it known *at first*- Not, he was certain, by his face. Admittedly he was quite pale, but in London, in winter, most people are pale. Did it, perhaps, affect the way he walked? No—scent seemed the only way to account for it. His pursuer had smelled him out, like a truffle; it hunted him, as a hound a hare. 24, 22, 20, 18, 16. 16 was FOR SALE. He had only been to Temple Fortune once before, when he had been searching so desperately for a flat. He had looked at a rather commodious bedsitter on Ashbourne Avenue, but that had not been possible, as he would have had to share the bath. He had, even yet, more conscience than that. Could someone have seen him getting in or out of the tub at Portland Road, and reported it? Not, one would have supposed, with a window of frosted glass. And at work he never used the toilets, out of the same consideration. London lacked the customary air of *suspicion* of a Marrakesh or a Beirut. He must escape, he *had* to escape. Escape where? Back to Portland Road to pack? But what if one of those things was waiting there? In the closet. No, it would never have fit in the closet. Somewhere else. No, the risk was too great. He should have thought, during the day, to go to his bank. Too late. He shivered, remembering again its metronomic knock, remembered looking out the paranoid peep-hole he'd drilled in the door the day he'd moved in. Lucky that he had! Remembered the gray low bulk of it, like nothing so much as an overturned icebox. How had it got upstairs? Did it walk—or, which seemed likelier, use treads? He knew almost nothing of its capabilities. Was its seeming sluggishness a ruse? So that when it finally came close enough it could make a sudden, unanticipated spurt?

He must escape, but he was so tired. Two days and a night without sleep. He had to rest, but he dared not rest. He would cross the Channel and go north. To Denmark. Then Sweden. He would always be able to find some kind of light work. His chest hurt. He had never dared visit a London doctor with his cold, even at its worst. No matter what medicines he took, it lingered on. It was the cold that made him so giddy now, not ... the other thing. The cold and fear. Fear and weariness, a terrible weariness, so that he dared not even stand in a doorway and rest his eyes. He would have slept and the machine would have tracked him down, inexorably. Where would it be now? Somewhere along the Finchley Road, no doubt, sniffing after him the way he'd come on the bus. He'd reached the corner of the block, a green-grocer's, and, opposite, a dairy that was just closing. And here he had thought the time nearly midnight! He squinted at the street sign above the greengrocer's awn-ing. This was the corner of Finchley Road and Ash-bourne Avenue. He'd come full circle on himself! The light in the dairy was switched off. He leaned back against the cold glass of the greengrocer's door and stared at the car parked before him, its windows opaque with frost. It had been such a warm winter until just last week, and he had been grateful for that, since he was unable, now, to wear woollen clothes. His chest hurt and his legs hurt. He crossed the street and walked down Finchley Road until he found a turning to the left. He turned left. He walked past rows and rows of identi-cal Tudor houses, and in each of them lived an identical Tudor king. He was hungry, he needed to sleep, and his chest hurt. He would go to Sweden, though he couldn't speak Swedish. Someone had told him that every Swede spoke English as a second language. He knew Arabic though, for all the good that would do him! How had they let him get through Customs? To have come so far, to have come so close, and now ... The street ended, and there was nothing but a vacancy. Had he come as far south as the Heath? A hill, trees. The sky's under-belly, livid with electric light. Soon, with the new mirrors being orbited, London would be bathed in an eternal day. The birds would stay awake all through the night, flowers would forget to close their blossoms. He remembered the devastated slopes of the Atlas mountains, the maddened villagers. He was leaning against the trunk of a tree, sheltered by the bare branches. The joint between his skull and the upper vertebrae ached and creaked as though in need of lubrication. He allowed his eyes to close. He had known all along really that his flight was useless. Already at the foot of the hill he saw it—an overturned icebox. It approached at an even, slow speed over the frozen ground, following exactly the path he had taken. It had come this close in Camden Town, and yet he had escaped it then. He could still . . . No. Just as a suicide will undress before entering the water, he unbuttoned his overcoat and let it slip from his shoulders. The machine paused two feet from him. One motor ceased its purring, another sprang to life, but there was, between these sounds, a brief, hallowed silence. The blunt forepart of the machine began to lift up, and he thought he could see, through the grid that covered it, tiny electric lights flickering within. When it was fully upright, it was a foot and a half shorter than him. The telescoping limbs began to strip away his cotton suit, quickly but with gentleness. The protective plates slid aside to reveal the main compartment, and for the first time he could see its huge rubber lips. Then, inexorably, the rubber lips kissed the leper's open sores.

Foreword to THE LAST HURRAH OF THE GOLDEN HORDE

I'm not going to have the limitless gall to attempt an appraisal of my own work; rather, I'd like to explain why I put "The Last Hurrah of the Golden Horde" in this book, and what writing the story meant to me.

To begin, Jerry Cornelius is Michael Moorcock's synthetic myth-figure, as I've explained earlier, and as I've also indicated, other writers have written "Jerry Cornelius stories" with Moorcock's enthusiastic encouragement and at his instigation. Among them have been Brian W. Aldiss, James Sallis, and M. John Harrison. Needless to say, there is more to the Jerry Cornelius story than a particular character and mythic structure, or all of these writers who are more than capable of creating their own characters and structures would never have written the things.

All of Moorcock's Jerry Cornelius stories, except "The Final Programme" in which the basic myth is outlined, have an illusive surface, consisting of actions, emotions, and premonitions described from weird off-angles. The basic Cornelius myth is shoved into the background as an unexamined assumption, and the stories consist entirely of variations, experiments in prose form, surface, and style. This is why other writers have tried their hand at Jerry Cornelius stories, not so much out of fascination with the subject matter, but in an attempt to learn from the experience of writing this sort of fiction.

Some Cornelius stories are similar to Moorcock's stories in content and style, some are less so. What I was interested in was neither the content as such nor exactly the style, but the revolutionary off-angle of attack. I've used Cornelius-as-assassin, which is part of the mythos, but nothing else of the Cornelius subject matter. Instead I've substituted some contemporary mythic elements which are the common property of all of us, figuring that these should work at least as well as the synthetic Cornelius myth. Actually, I had most of this story in my head before I ever heard of Jerry Cornelius; I had everything but a central character and a point of view. The story seemed to require the absence of a central character and his presence at the same time; thus using a somewhat irrelevant character out of a different story seemed the ideal solution. I made no attempt to imitate Moorcock's style, but I did try to understand the approach which, when combined with his own idiosyncracies as a writer of prose, created that style. I had access to Cornelius stories by several other writers who generated their own "Cornelius styles" but with different flavors of prose, and their example helped to extract the basic attack from all the unessentials.

All this may sound like an abstruse and complex explanation of a story that is essentially a piece of humor, but personally I feel that I learned more about the nature of form, attack, and style from writing "The Last Hurrah of the Golden Horde" than from any other story I've ever written. And despite the complex analysis that went into the writing of it, I had a hell of a lot of fun writing this story.

THE LAST HURRAH

OF THE

GOLDEN HORDE

by Norman Spinrad

Eastward across the Gobi, three hundred old men ride upon three hundred shaggy, wizened Mongolian ponies. The ponies, like their riders, are the tag-end of a dying breed. The men are dressed in filthy, cracked, badly tanned leathers. Across their backs are strapped short Mongolian bows; swords dangle from their waists and they carry lances in their horny hands as they ride toward the sunrise.

In the dingy storefront on Sullivan Street identified as the D'Mato Social Club by the peeling green letters on the fly-specked translucent area above the black-painted area of the plate glass window that hid the cave-like interior from the view of casual assassins in the street, Jerry Cornelius, a not-so-casual (or in his own way a *more* casual) assassin, sat on a gray-enamelled metal folding chair facing a gnarled old man with a Jimmy Durante nose across the cracked surface of a rickety card-table. Jerry wore a carefully dated black suit, a black silk shirt, a white tie, and white boots. His black vinyl raincoat was draped across a counter which paralleled one wall of the room and which held a display of candy bars and a cardboard showcase of De Nobili cigars. Behind the counter hung a faded photograph of Franklin D. Roosevelt framed in black. The man with the Jimmy Durante nose was smoking a De Nobili and the semi-poisonous smoke that he blew across the table was clearly designed to blow Jerry's cool. Jerry, however, had expected this, and as a counter-measure kept his violin case close at hand. It seemed a draw.

"This is a big one, Cornelius," the old man said.

"Flesh is flesh, Mr. Siciliano," Jerry replied. "Metal is metal."

"Have you ever hit a Cabinet-level official before?"

Jerry pondered. "It's open to doubt," he finally admitted. "I got a head of state once, but it was a benevolent despotism."

The old man chewed his cigar, much to Jerry's disgust. "It'll have to do," he said. "You've got the contract. How soon can you be in Sinkiang?"

"Three days. I'll have to change passports again."

"Make it two."

"I'd have to pull strings. It'll cost you."

The old man shrugged. "Do it," he said.

Jerry grinned. "My motto, Mr. Siciliano. Who's the contract on?"

"Mao Tze Tung's heir apparent."

"Who's that these days?" Jerry asked. The situation in China had gotten somewhat muddled.

"That's your problem," Durante-nose said.

Jerry shrugged. "And my cover?"

"Arrange it yourself."

Jerry got up clutching his violin case, ran his hand through his great bush of blond natural, retrieved his raincoat, took a De Nobili from the counter, and said with an evil smirk: "Don't say I didn't warn you."

* * *

The railroad train consisted of a locomotive, a sealed boxcar, three flatcars and a caboose. The boxcar contained one ton of (uncut?) heroin. The open flatcars held three hundred members of the People's Army of China armed with machine guns, protected from the elements by the thought of Chairman Mao. The caboose held the negotiating team. The locomotive was a diesel job.

"You'll be working with the Russians on this, Inspector Cornelius," Q said. "Our interests happen to coincide."

Jerry frowned. The last time he had worked with a Russian, he had contracted the clap. "I don't trust those buggers," he told Q.

"Neither do we," Q said crisply, "but it's the only way we can get you into Sinkiang. You leave for Moscow on Aeroflot in the morning."

"Aeroflot?" whined Jerry. Christ, those Russian stewardesses! he thought. "I get airsick on Aeroflot," he complained.

Q glared at Jerry firmly. "We're getting the family plan discount," he explained.

"But I'm flying alone. . . ."

"Precisely."

"Dramamine?"

"If you insist," Q said primly. "But the Bureau frowns on foreign substances."

"My mission?" Jerry asked.

"Catch the Chinks and the Maf in the act. Bust them."

"But we have no jurisdiction."

"Hence the Russians," said Q. "Use your head, Cornelius."

"They have no jurisdiction either."

"You're not that naive, Cornelius."

"I suppose not," Jerry said wistfully.

* * *

According to the thoughts of Chairman Mao, the village was an anachronism: one hundred and fifty-three flea-bitten nomads, along with their animals (mostly diseased horses and threadbare yaks) encamped in a cluster of leather yurts on the margin of the Gobi. From the correct point of view, the village might be said not to exist.

From this same point of view (as well as from several others) the three hundred old men who galloped in from the wastes of the Gobi might also be said to be nonexistent. Nevertheless, the nomad encampment had a certain reality for the old warriors; in fact an archetypal reality stretching back in a line of unbroken tradition from the days of the Great Khan and his Golden Horde still burning clearly in their ancestral memory to the misty and arthritic present.

Village. Burn. Pillage. Rape. Kill.

Outside the umbrella of the thoughts of Chariman Mao, the old barbarians existed in a happier reality of simple, straightforward traditional imperatives.

Therefore, unmindful of the fact that the village was an anachronism, the old warriors, in the time-honored tradition of the Golden Horde, rode into the encampment, slew the men and children, made a pass at raping the women to death, slaughtered the animals, burned the yurts, and continued to ride eastward, secure in the knowledge that they had fulfilled another quantum of their timeless destiny.

A long concrete runway broke the monotony of the Sinkiang wastelands with the more absolute monotony of its geometric perfection. At right angles to the runway, a railroad spur wandered off toward the horizon. From the viewpoint of the pilot of the C-5A approaching this three-dimensional nexus, the runway and the railroad spur formed a T with a finite bar and an infinite upright. If anything, the pilot thought this sloppy. It is likely that he did not fully comprehend the thoughts of Chairman Mao; a more erudite man might have appreciated the symbolism.

"It is a clear demonstration of the cynical perfidy of the Chinese gangster element enshrined behind the facade of the Maoist clique, Comrade Cornelius," Commissar Krapotkin observed genially, drawing a glass of tea from the silver samovar and handing it across the table to Jerry. Krapotkin was a short barrel of a man who wore his double-breasted Mod suit like a uniform. Perhaps it is a uniform, Jerry thought, as he took a spiked sugar cube out of his mother-of-pearl pillbox and inserted it between his teeth. The Russians were doing their best to be hip these days and it was hard to keep up.

As Jerry sipped tea through the sugar cube between his teeth, Krapotkin lit up an Acapulco Gold and continued to make small talk: "While they gibber and squeak their anti-Soviet obscenities in Peking, they deal with the worst gangster element of the decadent capitalist society by their back door in Sinkiang, which, by the way, is of course rightfully Soviet territory."

"I wouldn't call the Maf the *worst* gangster element of decadent capitalist society," Jerry observed mildly.

Krapotkin produced a metallic sound which Jerry tentatively identified as a laugh. "Ah, very good, Comrade Cornelius. Indeed, one might argue that the distribution of heroin, contributing as it does to the further corruption of the already decadent West, is an act which contributes to the long range progress of the working class."

"But providing the reactionary adventurist regime in Peking with hard American currency does not," Jerry rejoined.

"Exactly, Comrade! Which is why my government has decided to cooperate with the American narcs.

Once the Maoist clique has been exposed in the act of selling heroin to the Maf, we should have no trouble totally discrediting them with progressive elements throughout the world."

"And of course the Mafia will be discredited as well."

"?"

"The Maf is essentially a patriotic organization like the K.K.K. or the Loyal Order of Moose."

Krapotkin roached his joint. "Enough of the pleasantries, Comrade," he said. "Are you prepared for the drop?"

Jerry fingered his violin case. "My cover?" he inquired.

"You will be a Mafia hit man assigned a contract on the heir apparent to Mao Tze Tung," Krapotkin said. "Our agents in Palermo have uncovered just such a plot."

"The real hit man?"

Krapotkin smiled. "He has been disposed of, I assure you."

From a certain viewpoint, Jerry reflected, Krapotkin was right.

Not ninety seconds after the C-5A had taxied to a halt with its tail facing the juncture of the rail-spur-runway T as if preparing to fart along the track, the great doors in the nose opened like the petals of an aluminum flower, a ramp was lowered, and a black Cadillac disgorged, pulling a house trailer of grandiose proportions and Miami-Beach-Gothic design. The C-5A continued to disgorge Cadillacs like a pregnant guppy, each one pulling a trailer larger and more rococo than the last.

Something less than three hundred old men galloped haltingly across the wastes of Sinkiang on faltering ponies. A dozen or more of the Mongol warriors had burst blood vessels in their tired old brains from the excitement of the last massacre. The blood was running thin. Where once the steppes had echoed to the pounding hooves of the Golden Horde as the whole world trembled before a tide of barbarians that filled the field of vision from horizon to horizon, now there was naught but an expiring handful of decrepit savages. *Sic transit gloria mundi.* The spirit was willing, but the flesh was practically moribund. The survivors envied those few of their comrades lucky enough to have died a warrior's death sacking the last village in an endless chain reaching back to the glory days when the villages had names like Peking and Samarkand and Damascus.

But something—call it pride or manly virtue—kept the pitiful remnant of the Horde going, riding ever eastward into the sunrise. Perhaps it was the hope that somewhere on the endless steppe there still remained a village large enough (but not *too* large) to bring them all the glory of death in one last gory, triumphant, final massacre. Flailing like tattered battle flags in their befuddled old brains the simple imperatives which shaped their lives and hopes and destinies: Village. Burn. Pillage. Rape. Kill.

Jerry Cornelius, still clutching the violin case, stood alone in the gray wasteland, and watched the Russian helicopter disappear into the slate-colored sky with a certain sense of foreboding. You just can't trust those Russians, he thought. Now where was the car?

To the east was a large boulder. Behind it, and not without a certain sense of relief, Jerry found a late model black Cadillac sedan, well waxed and shiny. So far, so good.

Inside the car, Jerry found his new persona. Doffing his clothes, he assumed the persona: a black pin-striped suit with pegged pants and thin lapels, a white button-down shirt, a white tie, a diamond stickpin, pointed black Italian loafers, argyle socks, a box of De Nobilis, and jars of black shoe polish and vaseline, with which he gave himself a Rudolph Valentino job, atop which he affixed a green porkpie hat with a leopard skin band. Thus accoutered, and with a round toothpick in his mouth at a jaunty angle, he sealed the car, turned on the air-conditioning, and set out across the wasteland.

Only when he discovered that the radio would bring in nothing but Radio Moscow and that the tape library contained naught but Tchaikovsky did the full extent of Krapotkin's treachery become apparent.

As the train hove into sight of the rail-spur-runway junction, the soldiers of the People's Army were able to contain cries of awe, amazement and dismay only by diligent application of the thoughts of Chairman Mao.

For there in the depths of Sinkiang was, considering the circumstances, quite a decent facsimile of Las Vegas. A semicircle of trailers rimmed a large kidney-shaped swimming pool. Done up in pastels, sporting picture windows, and sprouting numerous extensions, wings, and breezeways, the trailers resembled the lower or casino floors of Las Vegas hotels. Complex mazes of cabanas, beach chairs, bocci courts, pavilions, greenhouses, handball courts and pigeon coops which filled the interstices between the trailers completed the illusion. Behind the semicircular Las Vegas facade towered the tail of the C-5A, reminiscent, somehow, of Howard Hughes and all that his shadowy persona implied. Parked among the spectral casino hotels were an indeterminate number of black Cadillacs.

Around the pool, waiters in red tuxedoes served tepid Collinses to fat men in sunglasses stretched out in beach chairs, warming themselves with complex arrays of sunlamps. Starlets in bikinis paraded their pinchable asses by the poolside.

The officials in the caboose immediately called for

182

the reserve train which had been parked fifty miles down the track in anticipation of such a necessity.

Approaching his destination from the south, Jerry Cornelius spotted a cluster of pagodas, huts and barracks, among which huge billboards had been erected bearing immense portraits of Mao, Lenin, Stalin, Enver Hoxha, and other popular personalities of the People's Republic of China. Everything was festooned with calligraphy like a wedding cake. Intermittent strings of firecrackers exploded. Hatchet men chased each other through the winding streets. Soldiers of the People's Army performed calisthenics. The sharp syllables of Chinese dialects filled the air like razor blades. Gongs sounded. Paper dragons danced in the streets. Perpetual twilight hovered over the scene, which, upon closer inspection, proved to be constructed of balsa wood, rice paper and paper mache.

Warily, Jerry swung the Cadillac wide of this Chinese version of Disneyland and circled toward the tail of a C-5A which dominated the landscape. Soon reality (such as it was) changed and he found himself on the outskirts of what appeared to be a suburb of Las Vegas: the lower stories of casino hotels mounted on wheels and parked in a semicircle around a huge kidney-shaped pool, facing the Chinese apparition across the chlorinated waters.

Having spied a heavily guarded boxcar behind the facade of the Chinese reality, Jerry was not surprised to see a dozen thugs with machine guns guarding the C-5A. The $50,000,000 must be on the plane.

For a moment, Jerry parked the Cad along the Orient-Vegas interface, playing at pondering his next move.

Shortly, he drove on into the Mafia camp, parked the Cadillac next to a fire hydrant outside a barbershop, and melted into the scene with barely a ripple. Yes indeed, this was his kind of town!

Eastward across the wastelands, here and there a rider dead on his horse, a scungy pony faltering under its rider, the spirit burning brighter as the blood thinned as if their ancient flesh were ectoplasmating into naught but the weathered parchment-dry quintessence of tradition-cum-desire, the desperate determination not to die a peasant's death, the image of the Final Massacre burning its forlorn hope into the backs of what was left of their arteriosclerotic brains, the husks of the Golden Horde doddered onward, ever onward.

"Ya get da Big Picture, Cornelius?" the Rock said, sipping at his Collins as he and Jerry lay side by side in beach chairs, sunning themselves at poolside. Jerry, dressed in neon-blue bathing suit, contrasting yellow terrycloth robe, Japanese rubber sandals and silvered Air Force shades, had resisted the dangerous urge to order Pernod, and as a consequence was nursing a foul rum concoction. Only the presence of his violin case close at hand soothed his jangled nerves. And the sun-lamps threatened to melt the shoepolish in his hair.

"I'm not paid to get the Big Picture, Rock," Jerry said, keeping in character, though from a certain viewpoint what he was saying was true.

The Rock scratched his hairy paunch with one hand and with the other, clawlike, pinched the ass of a passing starlet, who giggled appropriately.

"I like yer style, kid," the Rock said. "But doncha have any curiosity?"

"Curiosity killed a cat."

"I'm a dog man myself, Cornelius, so who gives a shit? What I say is dese Chinks have been asking for it. Just because da punks got a few H-bombs and ICBMs is no reason for them to get the idea they can burn the Maf and live ta talk about it. Yeah, after ya hit their number two *padron,* that smart-ass punk in Peking will have to look over his shoulder a few times before he tries putting milk-sugar in our heroin again."

"Just who is their number two?"

Rock pointed his De Nobili at the empty raft anchored out in the center of the kidney-shaped pool. "Da Big Boy will make this year's deal out on da raft—neutral turf. Whatever Chink is out there with him—zap!"

"Won't the Reds . . . ?" Jerry inquired.

"Da Cads are full of heavies with choppers." The Rock grinned. "When you hit da number two, dey hit da People's Army." The Rock chucked himself under the chin with his right forefinger as if flicking a bead of sweat at the giant posters of Mao, Stalin, Hoxha and Lenin glowering like spectral Internal Revenue agents across the moat-waters of the pool.

Jerry decided to develop a sudden hankering for Egg Foo Yung.

Major Sung passed the opium pipe across the black-lacquered table to Jerry, who inhaled the sweet smoke and fingered his violin case voluptuously as Major Sung caressed his copy of the Little Red Book obscenely and said: "Of course I am familiar with your work in England, Colonel Kor Ne Loos."

"Your English is excellent, Major," Jerry lied. "Harvard?"

"Berlitz."

"I should be reporting to the honorable Heir Apparent to godlike Mao," Jerry chided.

Major Sung frowned and kicked the brass gong which sat upon the table. Kung-fu, Jerry noted warily. He revised his estimate of Major Sung laterally. "As you of course know," Sung said with an oriental leer, "the peacock often hides his egg behind an embroidered fan."

Jerry started—he certainly hadn't expected anything like this! "The dragon has been known to preen his scales before he pounces," he rejoined.

Outside the pagoda, a chorus of two hundred kindergarten students were chanting the latest Number One on the Chinese Top 40, "Death To The Violaters Of The Spirit of Mao's Urine." Jerry tapped his fingers on the table in time to the catchy rhythm, which he recognized as a variation on "Rock Around The Clock."

"May I take that to imply that the pasta contains an asp?" Major Sung said. It was clearly not a question.

Jerry smiled. "As Confucius says, a fox with a dagger may behead a drunken lion."

Major Sung laughed. "As Chairman Mao has observed, the enemies of the Revolution will devour their own entrails if they can make a fast buck in the process."

Bowing and scraping, a Sergeant in a kimono entered the chamber with tea and fortune cookies.

Major Sung cracked open his pastry and read aloud: "Death to the revisionist running dogs of the Wall Street imperialists and their would-be lackeys in Prague."

Jerry's fortune cookie said: "Tension, apprehension and dissension have begun."

As Jerry, in his pin-stripe suit, porkpie hat, and Italian loafers, lounged against the right front fender of the Cadillac, which he had parked inconspicuously at poolside, a fat man in a flowered Hawaiian shirt and black Bermuda shorts boarded a speedboat at the Vegas end of the pool. Stuffed between his thick lips was an El Ropo Supremo Perfecto Grande. Set jauntily on his bald head was a red sailor cap on the brim of which "The Big Boy" had been embroidered in Atlantic City in bold blue thread.

As a Meyer Davis orchestra in one of the poolside cabanas struck up "Amore" and a stripper began to peel on the diving board, the white speedboat set out across the pool toward the raft.

Meanwhile across the pool, fifty soldiers of the People's Army marched back and forth bearing placards serializing the menu of Hong Fat's restaurant in severe calligraphy and psychedelic posters of Mao, Stalin, Lenin and Jim Morrison while the People's Army Brass Band played "Chinatown, My Chinatown" to which a chorus of Red Guards waving the Little Red Book sung the "Internationale" in Sinosized Albanian. To this heady send-off, an old bearded Chinese in a military tunic (with a curious if superficial resemblance to Ho Chi Minh) rowed a punt toward the raft in neutral waters.

At poolside, Jerry's trained eye picked out heavies in blue serge suits moving unobtrusively toward their Cadillacs. They all carried violin cases. Jerry placed a bet with a convenient bookie that the cases did not contain violins. The best he could get was the wrong end of 9-4 odds.

Alone on the raft at last, the Big Boy and the Heir Apparent swapped bon mots as the strains of "High Hopes" mingled with the thin voices of schoolchildren chanting "My Mao Can Lick Your Mao" in a corrupt Canton dialect.

"Ya dirty mother, last year's dope was cut with milk-sugar."

"As Chairman Mao has observed, when dealing with corrupt mercenaries of the exploitative class, the doctrine of 'no tickee, no washee' is fully justified."

"Remember what happened to Bugsy Siegal!"

"Confucius once said that a toothless dragon does not fear the orthodontist."

* * *

Behind the Chinese Disneyland, the People's Army had placed six machine gun nests in a circle around the boxcar of heroin.

Twenty heavies with choppers ringed the C-5A. Inside, five more heavies guarded $50,000,000 in unmarked small bills.

"Fifty million! That's robbery. You Chinks are crooks."

The Meyer Davis orchestra played "It Takes Two To Tango." The People's Army Brass Band countered with a Chinese version of "Die Fahne Hoch."

"As Chairman Mao has said," the Heir Apparent threatened, "I may not be the best man in town, but I'll be the best till the best comes round."

Hidden behind a facade of placards, posters, pagodas, dancing paper dragons, hatchet men, schoolchildren performing calisthenics, rioting Red Guards, captured American airmen in chains, opium dens and filthy peasant huts, three hundred soldiers of the People's Army of the People's Republic of China girded themselves for a human wave attack.

"We only deal with you Commie pinko Chink bastards because you're the only mass suppliers of heroin aside from the Federal narcs that we can find."

"As Chairman Mao has said, tough shit."

Ominously, the Meyer Davis orchestra began playing "Hawaiian War Chant."

Jerry Cornelius stubbed out his roach and reached for his violin case. "The time has come, the Walrus said, to speak of many things," he observed as, out on the raft, the Big Boy gave the finger to the Heir Apparent.

"Fifty million for the boxcar, take it or leave it," the Heir Apparent said.

The People's Army Brass Band broke into "Light My Fire" as seven hundred Red Guards doused themselves with gasoline and immolated themselves while singing "Chairman Mao ist unser Fuehrer" contrapuntally, but since they were all off-key, the ploy was a failure.

"As Al Capone once observed, play ball, or we lean on you."

Jerry Cornelius opened his violin case and withdrew a violin. To the untrained observer, it appeared to be merely an ordinary electric violin with self-contained power supply, built-in amp and speaker rated at 100 watts. However, an Underground electronics expert on 150 mg. of methedrene had made a significant modification: the high notes registered well into the ultrasonic and the lows were deep down in the subsonic, while all audible frequencies were eliminated.

When Jerry tucked the violin under his chin and began to play "Wipeout," the brains of everyone within a five mile radius began to vibrate to the beat of a drummer who was ultra-and-supersonic as well as different and nonexistent. To the naked human ear, Jerry appeared to be playing "The Sounds of Silence."

Out on the raft, the Big Boy was growing quite cross as the subliminal strains of "Wipeout" inflamed cells deep within his paretic brain. "Mao Tze Tung eats shit!" he informed the Heir Apparent.

"Al Capone was a faggot, according to the infallible thoughts of Mao Tze Tung!"

The Meyer Davis orchestra began to play "The Battle Hymn of the Republic."

The People's Army Brass Band immolated their tuba player.

As Jerry segued into a subliminal rendition of "Heartbreak Hotel," fifty slot machines produced spontaneous jackpots, Cadillacs gunned their engines, whores' poodles howled, thirteen plate glass windows shattered, and every starlet at poolside achieved climax. (Some of them had not come since their first screen-tests.)

Hatchet men began chopping at paper mache pagodas. A paper dragon set itself on fire. Three hundred soldiers preparing themselves for a human wave attack began to drool and got erections. Seven hundred chanting kindergarten children achieved satori and began to devour an American flag drenched with soy sauce. A giant poster of Stalin broke into a grin and thumbed its nose at a poster of Mao.

"Mao Tze Tung eats the hairy canary!"
"The Maf sucks!"
"Faggot!"
"Creep!"
"Chink!"
"Wop!"
"ARGH!"

Salivating, the Big Boy leapt at the Heir Apparent, chomping his El Ropo Supremo Perfecto Grande to

190

bits, and buried teeth and cigar in the old Chinaman's beard, setting it aflame. The two men wrestled on the raft, biting, spitting and cursing for a few moments, then toppled each other into the pool, which proved to be filled with crocodiles.

Pleased with his work, Jerry Cornelius began to play "Fire."

A phalanx of Cadillacs screamed around the pool and barreled into the People's Army Brass Band spewing machine gun bullets which ripped into a poster of Mao Tze Tung, enraging a rioting mob of Red Guards who set themselves on fire and threw themselves under the wheels of the cars, causing them to skid into a balsa wood pagoda which toppled into the pool in splinters which were devoured by the blood-crazed crocodiles who expired in agony from the splinters in their stomachs some time later.

Three hundred soldiers of the People's Army launched a human wave attack, firing their machine guns at random.

Jerry continued to play "Fire," seeing no particular reason to change the tune.

Major Sung shrieked: "Capitalistic running dogs of the demographic People's revisionist lackeys of Elvis Presley have over-run the ideological manifestations of decadent elements within the amplifier of the pagoda!" and committed hara-kiri.

* * *

The Rock began smashing slot machines with a baseball bat.

Starlets tore off their bikinis and chased terrified hatchet men around the poolside.

The human wave reached the pool, dove in, and proceeded to beat moribund crocodiles to death with their gunbutts.

A suicide squad hurled itself through the plate glass window of a trailer and devoured the rug.

Cadillacs circled the boxcar of heroin like hostile Indians, filling the air with hot lead.

The sopping remnants of the human wave reached the trailer camp and began beating thugs to death with dead crocodiles.

Red Guards showered the C-5A with ink bottles.

Tongues of flame were everywhere.

Explosions, contusions, fire, gore, curses, looting, rape.

Jerry Cornelius began playing "All You Need Is Love," knowing that no one was listening.

* * *

Riding eastward across the wastelands on their diseased ponies, something under two hundred decrepit remnants of what once had been the glorious Golden Horde, most of them incoherent with exhaustion, spied a great conflagration on the horizon.

Flaccid adrenals urged near-moribund hearts to beat faster. They flayed their ponies with the shafts of their spears. Drool flecked the lips of doddards and ponies alike. Their backbrains smelled blood and fire in the air.

The smells of gunpowder, gasoline, burning balsa wood and paper mache, sizzling flesh, gave Jerry Cornelius a slight buzz as he began to play "Deck the Halls With Boughs of Holly." The swimming pool was colored a bright carnelian, which did little to mask the chlorine odor. Bits of anodized aluminum struggled to keep afloat amid scraps of charred balsa wood and shards of placards.

A dented Cadillac careened through a barricade of beach chairs and into a squad of Chinese soldiers beating a starlet to death with copies of the Little Red Book before sliding over the rim of the pool to sink bubbling into the churning depths.

The pillar of fire consuming the Chinese Disneyland reminded Jerry of the Dresden firestorm. Sentimentally, he began to play "Bongo, Bongo, Bongo, I Don't Want To Leave The Congo."

In a strange display of gallantry, Red Guards, hit men, capo mafiosos and Chinese soldiers joined hands in a ring around the ruined trailer camp, screaming *"Burn,* baby, burn!" in English, Mandarin, Cantonese, Italian Pidgin, and Yiddish. At each *"burn"* a canister of napalm dropped from somewhere onto the conflagration.

Reduced to sentimentality despite himself, Jerry played "God Save The Queen."

Two hundred or so pairs of rheumy eyes lit up with

feral joy at the sight of a great city (by current Horde standards anyway) going up in flames, at the sight of smashed cars, broken bodies, naked starlets shrieking, and a great pool of what appeared to be blood.

Weeping great nostalgic tears, the last generation of the Golden Horde shouldered their spears, whipped their ponies into a stumbling gallop and charged in a body into the fray, the image of the Final Massacre burning like a city in the fevered brains of the aged savages:

Village! Burn! Pillage! Rape! Kill!

Mongolian ponies wheezing and gasping under them, the crazed doddards reached the conflagration and found to their chagrin that there was precious little unburnt, unpillaged, unraped, unkilled.

They found a boxcar guarded by machine gunners and charged it en masse sacrificing half their number to impale the befuddled Chinese troops on their spears and set the boxcar aflame. As a strangely intoxicating aromatic smoke billowed from the burning boxcar, the remnant of the remnant scattered, looking for more things or people to burn, rape, and kill.

A dozen of the doddards expired attempting to rape an aged whore to death, and another dozen were compelled to shamefacedly trample her to death under the hooves of their ponies, eight of which expired from the effort.

Fifteen of the Horde had heart attacks trying to beat Cadillacs to death.

A half-dozen doddards died of broken hearts when the slot machines they were torturing failed to cry out in pain.

Several of the Horde fell to devouring the corpses of crocodiles and choked to death on the splinters.

* * *

As the last Khan of the Golden Horde watched in se-nile befuddlement, the great silver bird issued a terrible battle-cry and began to move. The doddard's bleary eyes bugged as the C-5A picked up speed, shot by him, and actually left the ground!

A feeble nervous impulse travelled spastically from his optic nerve into his brain, and thence to his arm and throat.

"Kill!" he wheezed asthmatically, and hurled his spear at the unnatural thing.

The spear was sucked into the intake of the left in-board jet engine, lodged in the turbine, and shattered it. The jet engine exploded, shearing off the wing. The C-5A nearly completed a loop before it crashed upside down to the runway and exploded into flames.

From an aerial viewpoint, the runway and the railroad spur formed a T with a finite bar and an infi-nite upright, but the only living being in the area did not notice the symbolism. Riding into the sunset on his pony, his back to what in the distance seemed naught but a smoldering refuse-heap, the last Khan of the Golden Horde, sole survivor of the Final Massacre, filled his dying brain with one thought, like a dwindling chord: fulfillment; Golden Horde died in glory; village; burned; pillaged; raped; killed; ancestors proud.

This thought flared brightly in his brain like a dying ember and then he went to that Great Carnage Heap in the Sky. The wheezing pony tripped over a rock, dis-lodging the body, which fell to the ground in a twisted heap. A vulture descended, pecked at the body, sniffed, and departed.

The pony staggered on for a few steps, then halted, its dim brain perhaps mesmerized by the glare of the setting sun.

* * *

The Mongolian pony was still standing there an hour later when Jerry Cornelius, in his pin-stripe suit, pork-pie hat, and Italian loafers, wandered dazedly up to it out of the wasteland.

"Here's a bit of luck," Jerry muttered, perking up a bit. (The short-circuiting of his electric violin had seriously vexed him.)

Jerry mounted the pony, kneed its flanks and shouted: "Git 'em up, Scout!

The pony waddled forward a few steps, puked, and died.

Jerry extricated himself from the corpse, brushed himself off, and consulted a fortune cookie he had secreted in a pocket.

"It's a long way to Tipperary," the fortune cookie informed him.

Munching the soggy rice pastry, Jerry trudged off into the setting sun whistling, "Dem bones, dem bones, dem dry bones, now hear de word of de Lord. . . ."

Foreword to
DOWN THE UP ESCALATION

Brian W. Aldiss is that rarest of beings in the field of speculative fiction, a mature writer who has lived up to his early bright promise and then some, expanding his horizons outward and inward while refining his sensibilities and gaining full mastery of prose and form.

His early stories and novels were more or less straightforward science fiction approached from more or less traditional points of view. But steadily, almost measuredly, his work evolved, becoming ever more sophisticated in sensibility, varied in form, adventuresome in prose, idiosyncratic in content. Novels like *The Dark Light-Years,* and *Greyhound* are truly novels in the most rigorous sense of the word, while remaining within the traditions of speculative fiction, an uncommon achievement in itself.

Three of his most recent novels give ample demonstration not only of Aldiss' achievements within the realm of speculative fiction but of his ability to hold his own and more in the world of literature at large. (Where, by the way, he is literary editor of the *Oxford Mail.*)

Report on Probability A is an overtly experimental novel, a conscious attempt to write a kind of speculative phenomenological novel, inspired by trends in modern French fiction. As such, it is more of a writer's novel than a reader's novel, designed more to extend the art than to reach a wide audience. On the other hand, his mainstream novel about boyhood, *The Hand-Reared Boy,* was a best-seller in England, lest anyone think that Aldiss has become a mandarin.

But the most ambitious of his recent works, in fact possibly the most ambitious speculative novel ever written, is *Barefoot in the Head.* Here Aldiss takes us on a trip (in the word's several meanings) through a Europe bombed back to the stoned age during the Acid Head War, where everyone drifts in and out of visionary states of various flavors and time has become silly putty. The book is written in an incredibly rich and dense prose full of Joycean punning and interpenetrations of time-loci in a genuinely post-Einsteinian temporality. It is a difficult book to read, but unlike most difficult books, you feel that your effort has been amply rewarded. It is surely a landmark in speculative fiction, perhaps even in world literature.

"Down the up Escalation" represents Aldiss' later short fiction in its complexity and maturity, in its interpenetration of levels which unite in a whole. Even in his short fiction, Aldiss is very much a novelistic writer, in fact one of the most novelistic speculative writers around.

Brian Aldiss' large body of speculative fiction displays a scope and steady growth unique in the literature. In the sense of having written more and more varied solid, interesting, venturesome speculative fiction than anyone else around, Aldiss must be considered the dean of speculative writers. But best of all, he has not retired behind the stone wall of his achievements to turn out endless replicas of his own successes. A fully matured writer, his work is nevertheless still reaching out, still growing, still expanding, still in a sense perpetually youthful. And that is the fullest maturity of all.

DOWN THE UP ESCALATION

by Brian W. Aldiss

Being alone in the house, not feeling too well, I kept the television burning for company. The volume was low. Three men mouthed almost soundlessly about the Chinese role in the Vietnam war. Getting my head down, I turned to my aunt Laura's manuscript.

She had a new hairstyle these days. She looked very good. she was seventy-three, my aunt, and you were not intended to take her for anything less: but you could mistake her for ageless. Now she had written her first book—'a sort of autobiography,' she told me when she handed the bundle over. Terrible apprehension gripped me. I had to rest my head in my hand. Another heart atack coming.

On the screen, figures scrambled over mountain. All unclear. Either my eyesight going or a captured Chinese newsreel. Strings of animals—you couldn't see what, film slightly overexposed. Could be reindeer crossing snow, donkeys crossing sand. I could hear them now, knocking, knocking, very cold.

A helicopter crashing toward the ground? Manuscript coming very close, my legs, my lips, the noise I was making.

There was a ship embedded in the ice. You'd hardly know there was a river. Snow had piled up over the piled-up ice. Surrounding land was flat. There was music, distorted stuff from a radio, accordions and balalaikas. The music came from a wooden house. From its misty windows, they saw the ship, sunk in the rotted light. A thing moved along the road, clearing away the day's load of ice, ugly in form and movement. Four people sat in the room with the unpleasant music; two of them were girls in their late teens, flat faces with sharp eyes; they were studying at the university. Their parents ate a salad, two forks, one plate. Both man and woman had been imprisoned in a nearby concentration camp in Stalin's time. The camp had gone now. Built elsewhere, for other reasons.

The ship was free of ice, sailing along in a sea of mist. It was no longer a pleasure ship but a research ship. Men were singing. They sang that they sailed on a lake as big as Australia.

"They aren't men. They are horses!" My aunt.

"There are horses aboard."

"I certainly don't see any men."

"Funny-looking horses."

"Did you see a wolf then?"

"I mean, more like ponies. Shaggy. Small and shaggy. Is that gun loaded?"

"Naturally. They're forest ponies—I mean to say, not ponies but reindeer. 'The curse of the devil,' they call them."

"It's the bloody rotten light! They do look like reindeer. But they must be men."

"Ever looked one in the eye? They are *the* most frightening animals."

My father was talking to me again, speaking over the phone. It had been so long. I had forgotten how I loved him, how I missed him. All I remembered was that I had gone with my two brothers to his funeral; but that must have been someone else's funeral, someone else's father. So many people, good people were dying.

I poured my smiles down the telephone, heart full of delight, easy. He was embarking on one of his marvellous stories. I gulped down his sentences.

"That burial business was all a joke—a swindle. I collected two thousand pounds for that, you know, Bruce. No, I'm lying! two and a half. It was chicken feed, of course, compared with some of the swindles I've been in. Did I ever tell you how Ginger Robbins and I got demobbed in Singapore at the end of the war, 1945? We bought a defunct trawler off a couple of Chinese businessmen—very nice old fatties called Pee —marvellous name! Ginger and I had both kept our uniforms, and we marched into a transit camp and got a detail of men organized—young rookies, all saluting us like mad—you'd have laughed! We got them to load a big LCT engine into a five-tonner, and we all drove out of camp without a question being asked, and—wham! —straight down to the docks and our old tub. It was boiling bloody hot, and you should have seen those squaddies sweat as they unloaded the engine and man-handled..."

"Shit, Dad, this is all very funny and all that," I said, "but I've got some work to do, you know. Don't think I'm not enjoying a great reminiscence, but I have to damned work, see? OK?"

I rang off.

I put my head between my hands and—no, I could not manage weeping. I just put my head between my hands and wondered why I did what I did. Subconscious working, of course. I tried to plan out a science fiction story about a race of men who had only subconsciouses. Their consciousnesses had been painlessly removed by surgery.

They moved faster without their burdening consciousnesses, wearing lunatic smiles or lunatic frowns. Directly after the operation, scars still moist, they had restarted World War II, some assuming the roles of Nazis or Japanese or Yugoslav partisans or British fighter pilots in kinky boots. Many even chose to be Italians, the role of Mussolini being so keenly desired that at one time there were a dozen Duces striding about, keeping company with the droves of Hitlers.

Some of these Hitlers later volunteered to fly with the Kamikazes.

Many women volunteered to be raped by the Wehrmacht and turned nasty when the requirements were filled. When a concentration camp was set up, it was rapidly filled; people have a talent for suffering. The history of the war was rewritten a bit. They had Passchendale and the Somme in; a certain President Johnson led the British forces.

The war petered out in a win for Germany. Few people were left alive. They voted themselves second-class citizens, mostly becoming Jewish negroes or Vietnamese. There was birching between consenting adults. These good folk voted unanimously to have their subconsciousnesses removed, leaving only their ids.

I was on the floor. My study. The name of the vinolay was—it had a name, that rather odious pattern of little wooden chocks. I had it on the tip of my tongue. When I sat up, I realized how cold I was, cold and trembling, not working very well.

My body was rather destructive to society, as the Top Clergy would say. I had used it for all sorts of things;

nobody knew where it had been. I had used it in an un-just war. Festival. It was called Festival. Terrible name, surely impeded sales.

I could not get up. I crawled across the floor toward the drink cupboard in the next room. Vision blurry. As I looked up, I saw my old aunt's manuscript on the table. One sheet had fluttered down on to the Festival. I crawled out into the dining room, through the door, banging myself as I went. Neither mind nor body was the precision ballistic missile it once had been.

The bottle. I got it open before I saw it was Sweet Martini, and dropped it. I rested my head in the mess.

"If I die now. I shall never read Aunt Laura's life . . ."

Head on carpet, bottom in air, I reached out and grasped the whisky bottle. Why did they make the stuff so hard to get at? Then I drank. It made me very ill indeed.

It was Siberia again, the dread reindeer sailing eternally their ships across the foggy icy lakes. They were munching things, fur and wood and bone, the saliva freezing into icicles as it ran from their jaws. Terrible noise, like the knocking of my heart.

I was laughing. Who ever died dreaming of reindeer —who but Lapps? Digging my fingers into the nameless carpet, I tried to sit up. It proved easier to open my eyes.

In the shady room, a woman was sitting. She had turned from the window to look at me. Gentle and reassuring lines and planes composed her face. It took a while to see it as a face; even as an arrangement against a window, I greatly liked it.

The woman came over to look closely at me. I realized I was in bed before I realized it was my wife. She touched my brow, making my nervous system set to

203

work on discovering whether the signal was a pain or pleasure impulse, so that things in there were too busy for me to hear what she was saying. The sight of her speaking was pleasurable; it moved me to think that I should answer her.

"How's Aunt Laura?"

The messages were coming through, old old learning sorting out speech, hearing, vision, tactile sensations, and shunting them through the appropriate organs. The doctor had been; it had only been a slight one, but this time I really would have to rest up and take all the pills and do nothing foolish; she had already phoned the office and they were very understanding. One of my brothers was coming round, but she was not at all sure whether he should be allowed to see me. I felt entirely as she did about that.

"I've forgotten what it was called."

"Your brother Bob?"

My speech was a little indistinct. I had a creepy feeling about whether I could move the limbs I knew were bundled with me in the bed. We'd tackle that challenge as and when necessary.

"Not Bob. Not Bob. The . . . the . . ."

"Just lie there quietly, darling. Don't try to talk."

"The . . . carpet . . ."

She went on talking. The hand on the forehead was a good idea. Irritably, I wondered why she didn't do it to me when I was well and better able to appreciate it. What the hell was it called? Roundabout?

"Roundabout . . ."

"Yes, darling. You've been here for several hours, you know. You aren't quite awake yet, are you?"

"Shampoo . . ."

"Later, perhaps. Lie back now and have another little doze."

"Variety . . ."

"Try and have another little doze."

* * *

One of the difficulties of being a publisher is that one has to fend off so many manuscripts submitted by friends of friends. Friends always have friends with obsessions about writing. Life would be simple—it was the secret of a happy life, not to have friends of friends. Supposing you were cast away on a desert island disc, Mr. Hartwell, what eight friends of friends would you take with you, provided you had an inexhaustible supply of manuscripts?

I leaned across the desk and said, "But this is worse than ever. You aren't even a friend of a friend of a friend, auntie."

"And what am I if I'm *not* a friend of a friend?"

"Well, you're an aunt of a nephew, you see, and after all, as an old-established firm, we have to adhere to certain rules of—etiquette, shall we call it, by which . . ."

It was difficult to see how offended she was. The pile of manuscript hid most of her face from view. I could not remove it, partly because there was a certain awareness that this was really the sheets. Finally I got them open.

"It's your life, Bruce. I've written your life. It could be a best-seller."

"Variety . . . No, Show Business . . ."

"I thought of calling it 'By Any Other Name'."

"We have to adhere to certain rules."

It was better when I woke again. I had the name I had been searching for: Festival. Now I could not remember what it was the name of.

The bedroom had changed. There were flowers about. The portable TV set stood on the dressing table. The curtains were drawn back and I could see into the garden. My wife was still there, coming over, smiling. Several times she walked across to me, smiling. The light came and went, the flowers changed position, color, the doctor got in her way. Finally she reached me.

"You've made it! You're marvellous!"

"You've made it! *You're* marvellous!"

No more trouble after that. We had the TV on and watched the war escalate in Vietnam.

Returning health made me philosophical. "That's what made me ill. Nothing I did . . . under-exercise, over-eating . . . too much booze . . . too many fags . . . just the refugees."

"I'll turn it off if it upsets you."

"No. I'm adapting. They won't get me again. It's the misery the TV sets beam out from Vietnam all over the world. That's what gives people heart attacks. Look at lung cancer—think how it has been on the increase since the war started out there. They aren't real illnesses in the old sense, they're sort of prodromic illness, forecasting some bigger sickness to come. The whole world's going to escalate into a Vietnam."

She jumped up, alarmed. "I'll switch it off!"

"The war?"

"The set."

The screen went blank. I could still see them. Thin women in those dark blue overalls, all their possessions slung from a frail bamboo over a frail shoulder. Father had died about the time the French were slung out. We were all bastards. Perhaps every time one of us died, one of the thin women lived. I began to dream up a new religion.

They had the angels dressed in U.N. uniform. They no longer looked like angels, not because of the uniform but because they were all disguised as a western diplomat—nobody in particular, but jocular, uneasy, stolid, with stoney eyes that twinkled.

My angel came in hotfoot and said, "Can you get a

206

few friends of friends together? The refugees are waiting on the beach."

There were four of us in the hospital beds. We scrambled up immediately, dragging bandages and sputum cups and bed pans. The guy next to me came trailing a plasma bottle. We climbed into the helicopter.

We prayed en route. "Bet the Chinese and Russian volunteers don't pray on the trip," I insinuated to the angel.

"The Chinese and Russians don't volunteer."

"So you make a silly insinuation, you get a silly innuendo," the plasma man said.

God's hand powered the chopper. Faster than engines but maybe less reliable. We landed on the beach beside a foaming river. Heat pouring down and up and sideways. The refugees were forlorn and dirty. A small boy stood hatless with a babe hatless on his back. Both ageless, eyes like reindeer's, dark, moist, cursed.

"I'll die for those two," I said, pointing.

"One for one. Which one do you choose?"

"Hell, come on now, angel, isn't my soul as good as any two Goddamned Viet kid souls?"

"No discounts here, bud. Yours is shop-soiled, anyway."

"OK, the bigger kid."

He was whisked instantly into the helicopter. I saw his dirty and forlorn face at the window. The baby sprawled screaming on the sand. It was naked, scabs on both knees. It yelled in slow motion, piddling, trying to burrow into the sand. I reached slowly out to it, but the exchange had been made, the angel turned the napalm on to me. As I fell, the baby went black in my shadow.

"Let me switch the fire down, if you're too hot, darling."

"Yuh. And a drink . . ."

She helped me struggle into a sitting position, put

207

her arm round my shoulders. Glass to lips, teeth, cool water in throat.

"God, I love you, Ellen, thank God you're not . . ."

"What? Another nightmare?"

"Not Vietnamese . . ."

It was better then, and she sat and talked about what had been going on, who had called, my brother, my secretary, the Roaches . . . "the Roaches have called . . ." "any Earwigs?" . . . the neighbors, the doctor. Then we were quiet awhile.

"I'm better now, much better. The older generation's safe from all this, honey. They were born as civilians. We weren't. Get me auntie's manuscript, will you?"

"You're not starting work this week."

"It won't hurt me. She'll be writing about her past, before the war and all that. The past's safe. It'll do me good. The prose style doesn't matter."

I settled back as she left the room. Flowers stood before the TV, making it like a little shrine.

FOREWORD TO CIRCULATION OF CONDENSED CONVENTIONAL STRAIGHT-LINE WORD-IMAGE STRUCTURES

Michael Butterworth is a young English writer who has carried speculative fiction to a new extreme in "Circularization." The entire piece is speculative in nature, not merely the content or even the prose or form, but the entire existence of the story as words on paper. There has been a certain amount of talk about "non-linear" writing of late, but here is a *really* non-linear work in the most rigorous sense.

"Circularization" is an experiment in perceptual psychology, among other things, and unlike most of this sort of "concrete prose," it seems to actually work. Here the reader is not merely passively reading speculative fiction, he is involved in the speculative element as an active participant. Whether the future of short fiction will be in this direction or not, "Circularization" is certainly a unique experience.

CIRCULARIZATION OF CONDENSED CONVENTIONAL STRAIGHT-LINE WORD-IMAGE STRUCTURES

(Radial-Planographic Condensed Word-Image Structures, Rotation about a Point)

by Michael Butterworth

Take:
I crossed the channel, Dover to Calais, in a motorboat.
I had a drink of tea on the way.
Condense:
Dover sea motortea—drink Calais
Take:
I crossed the channel, Dover to Calais, in a motorboat.
I had a talk about the war in Vietnam with a vicar, over a drink of tea.
Condense:
Dover. Vietnamese sea wartalk with motortea—drink vicar. Calais.
Rules For Reading Circularization Method
(1) Read Image-bars radially from circle origin outward toward circle periphery. Read round the circle, beginning at "solid bar" C (marked on diagram).

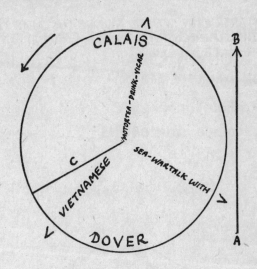

(2) Point A indicates "author's origin," or starting
point from for conveyance or fulfilment of idea or
narrative, to point B which is always the "author's
objective." In the circle, the author's origin is
DOVER. The author's objective is CALAIS. A always appears at the bottom of the circle, B always
at the top.

(3) Circle surface area may be printed with blue picture of sea (in this case), or with any other stock
subject (land, air, fire, etc.) relative to subject
matter in revolution.

(4) If more than one origin and objective is decided
upon by the author to fit a particular subject, then
the reader may expect to see a second or a third
"frame" (i.e. circle).

(5) Conversation, if required, is printed separately on
the page facing a frame.

211

(6) Familiarization with spontaneous, conscious interpretation of the condensed subject matter is important if the frames are to be read successfully.

NO TRUCE IN WHITE HOLOCAUSTMAS-TIME (YEAR OF CROSSING—1967)
by Michael Butterworth

Frame 1

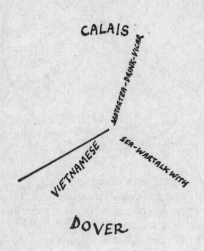

VICAR:
Against background noise of motorboat and sea. War, Vietcong soldiers, civilians, is an Image to be dealt with, not an attempt at facing Reality.
NARRATOR:
Ah, but what's Reality? Who can define that, Vicar?
VICAR:
I . . .

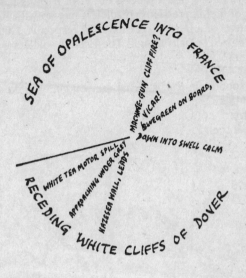

NARRATOR:
Against background noise of motorboat and sea. Ah, yes Reality! Those white cliffs. Good tea isn't it?

VICAR:
Oops! All over you. This reminds me of a long time ago, on the sea in a small boat. Or was it a book I'd been reading, about a hunch-back who operated a ferry service across the Channel? He used a rowing boat, by the way, and rescued trapped soldiers from the beaches at Dunkirk.

NARRATOR:
I can almost hear machine-gun fire coming from the cliffs. It's almost like Thomas Hardy now ...

VICAR:
Reality? We're over the board to phantasy in a minute!
Sound of machine-gun fire in the distance

VICAR:
Reality? In this case a process of . . . of friendly permutation of first impressions. If soldiers met up with Reality, instead of a false impression their respective Authority's "hatred" cloaks around The Enemy, soldiers would not fight.
NARRATOR:
We'll soon be in Calais. What are you going to do once we get there?
VICAR:
I have a friend . . .

Frame 3

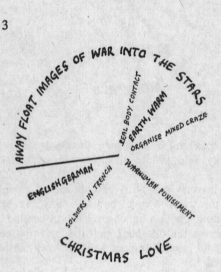

VICAR:
Against background noise of sea and boat. This is precisely what I mean. They're human now, true Christians, filled with spirit. At other times of the year they

fought one another. Can you believe it, seeing them so happy now? *Sounds of laughter and merriment coming from the trenches.* Christmas in Vietnam. You remember? They did the same thing.

NARRATOR:
At what cost? Look, if only you could, at my remembrances. There is a man . . .

Frame 4

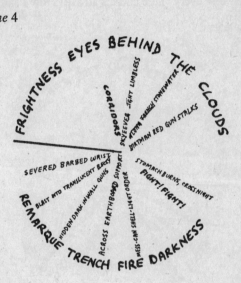

NARRATOR:
Against background noise of 1st WW machine guns, trench groans, sea and motorboat . . .
Now you see what I mean about War.

VICAR:
I see pain and suffering. I see no motive, only an exchange of senseless attacks. If men met in the flesh, instead of reading newspapers about one another, as they

did last Christmas time, they would soon learn *not* to hate one another. Because of a humanizing element that both sides have in common—a love of Father Christmas, if you like. Image of War, go away back into the clouds.

NARRATOR:

And of war? Isn't War just a *word*? We're getting onto very vaporous ground; here Vicar, finish your tea. Water water everywhere and it's all salt! How I suffer.

Frame 5

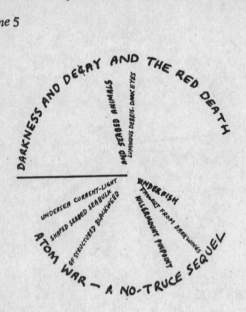

VICAR:

Ah the French coast, clearly at last. Listen to what they say—the white cliffs ten miles behind. *Very loud "rat-tat" of machine gun in echo chamber.* But there will be no question of post atomic survival. We'll have fought so much hatred to do that. It'll not be a question of slip-

ping across the "lines" to have a mixed party . . .
Enemy prejudice—false superboosted hatred Images—
won't exist. *Sound of motorboat and sea comes sudden-
ly into the foreground, as if the wind changes.*
VICAR:
Shouting above the noise.
I have a friend who runs a church in Versailles . . .

Frame 6

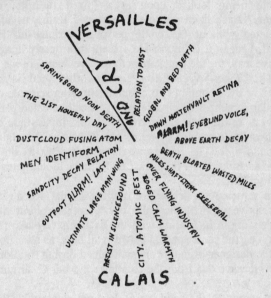

*Sound of motorboat and sea. In the distance, bells and
cannons from "1812 Overture." Silence*

NOTE AND EFFECTS ON AND OF CIRCULARI-
ZATION
by Michael Butterworth

The radial "spokes" of the straight-line word-image structures, revolving anticlockwise, have led me to term the effect: *"Radirote,"* from "radius" and "rotation." Radirote plural becomes "radirotii."

I have called the radirotii of the short passage *NO TRUCE IN WHITE HOLOCAUSTMAS-TIME* as representative of the *"Printed Frame Effect,"* each radirote being looked upon as a "fixed radirote, or frame." Each fixed radirote comprises 1 frame, usually depicted without the circle periphery printed-in. By fixed, I mean it is impossible, except in a purely imaginative way, for the Image-bars to revolve through time.

The *"Twin-Screen Effect,"* on the other hand, is arrived at by mounting two circular television screens, or similar screens, side by side on a vertically erected platform as in the diagram below. Here, the Image-bars of each radirote revolve or rotate about the circle's origin, *through time.* The Images would be broadcast as similarly as Images are broadcast on a conventional television screen.

In screen A (a "complete radirote frame" for direct descriptive report), the solid bar C rotates about the circle's origin in *fixation* with the fixed Image-bar rotation, i.e., the same spacing between all bars, as allocated by the designer or author, is maintained during rotation. The viewer reads from the rotating solid bar C, around the circle.

In screen B, the solid bar C does not rotate with the rest of the Image-bars. Instead C occupies a fixed position in relation to the screen, The Image-bars continue to rotate round the origin and go off the screen, appearing to merge into c, at point b in the diagram. Continuous (fresh) material comes onto the screen, appearing to revolve out of c, at point a. Such a radirote I have called a "continuous radirote frame," effective for "visual" observation of speech.

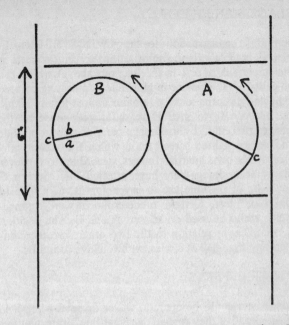

Operating Procedure: A commences bar rotation. B follows suit after time has been allowed for the audience to read the full bar content of A. Both revolve together. B revolves slower than A. When B reaches the end of its continuous effect, both radirotii cease bar rotation, and their images fade. After a pause of a few seconds, a fresh frame begins. A commences rotation, and their images fade. After a pause of a few seconds, a fresh frame begins. A commences rotation, etc.

The viewer glances quickly from screen to screen, absorbing the broadcast. Special, taped sound effects, sometimes necessary for each frame, are required. Viewer clamps a set of padded ear-phones to his head.

It is desirable for the audience to sit at a distance of at least fifteen feet from the screens, and to view in the dark, or in dim red lighting.

BLANK SCREEN EFFECT

Similar in construction to the TWIN-SCREEN EF-
FECT, but comprised also of a third screen (as large as
the screens A and B in the diagram above) which can
be called C. C gives neon-glow effect, pulsating colored
light and patterns, or else remains almost totally blank.
Its purpose is to give increased perception into the
Images presented by the Image-bars, or else to provide
an area of lighted screen upon which the viewer may
project his own internal Images, according to however
the rotating Image-bars have affected him. Screen C
could be of possible use to psychologists, as a type of
"ink-blot" test. Certain predetermined word-arrange-
ments could be used on screens A and B. The position
C occupies, in relation to the two other screens, com-
pletes a "triangle" of circles, with C above A and B.

OTHER EFFECTS

Image-bars could be made to waver or bend—i.e., it is
not imperative they remain "straight-line" in formation.
Image-bars could also be constituted of words having
varying letter-sizes, so that an intense depth-perception
into the screen could be achieved. This method takes
advantage of the fact that the viewer automatically re-
lates himself with the origin of the circle, no matter
what the screen he chooses to view.

What I call the "Original Effect" (not strictly concerned with radii-rotation), takes a similar advantage of
automatic autoidentity with the circle's center. Words
(of varying letter-sizes) are made to emerge from the
circle's origin on the screen. Their lettering in-
creases in size as they approach the periphery of the circle, and are free to follow whatever patterns and meanings have been given to them by designer or author. The
effect is that of a rush of words, appearing as if out of

"nothing," toward the viewer. At each rotation of the solid bar they change, and a fresh "frame" is begun.

LONG-TERM SIGNIFICANCE

What is the long-term significance of Circularization? It was originally devised by myself out of a belief that all processes in Nature (the perpetual deterioration of the Universe) are evolved out of (and make up) an infinite series of circles (or cycles).

An apparatus which is capable of giving the viewer actual "word experience," does not seem to me to be too much of a remote proposition to face. By "word experience" I mean *absolute appreciation of word significance to the viewer,* whereby the viewer becomes so much identified with a word that he virtually "lives in it" for a few moments, or rather "it may live" around him. Such an apparatus would necessarily involve stimulation of certain areas of the brain by electrodes. For instance it is possible, accidentally, for a person taking LSD to have just such "word experience," although whether in fact such a drug as LSD is "perfectly harmless" is debatable, and anyway it is not suitable (in its present structure) for the operation I have in mind. Certainly, I feel, the Circularization method of reading, in all its forms, is one step toward such an achievement. Using a "word experience" method though could enable children to "learn," in a few short sessions, the amount of data it normally takes a lifetime's study and experience to achieve. There is still a lot more research to be done.

Foreword to THE DEFINITION

The short-short, the story of under 1500 words, has been a staple of commercial science fiction. Usually these pieces have hinged on some sudden revelation at the end, have been shallow pieces of trickery, good for a laugh, or a wry grin, and not very much more. After all, how much can you do in 1500 words?

It is a measure of the growing maturity of speculative fiction, and the new mastery of its writers, that the short-short has undergone a renaissance of late. J.G. Ballard's so-called condensed novels are indeed miniature novels in terms of structure. Other writers have packed incredible amounts of feeling, imagery, and meaning into very short pieces. Density of prose and allusive imagery have enabled more sophisticated writers to turn what was once a "gimmick" form into high art.

In "The Definition," Bob Marsden, an Englishman who has written very little fiction, has almost written a miniature novel. Implicit in this very short piece is a whole future world and its evolution from our own time. Seldom have so few words done so much. It is this sort of speculative fiction that gives the lie to the fashionable notion in certain quarters that the short story is a moribund art form. The so-called mainstream short story may have played out all its variations, but mature speculative short fiction has hardly begun to explore the possibilities that have recently been opened up.

THE DEFINITION

by Bob Marsden

The night is old. The party, like the copulating couples in the corners, is breaking apart. Everybody looks tired and fucked out, none more so than Thriply Purblind and the Blinkers, who have raved mechanically throughout the night. Absently, Purblind observes the woman who hired him, flower suit flapping from the scaffolding of her gaunt body. She clicks and twitches, a puppet of articulated sticks dancing the Mantis. She is fifty-six years old. Today is her fortieth venereal birthday. She cries quietly as her body jerks: the fortieth anniversary of her first fuck, and it has brought nothing more than a couple of friendly but dutiful tickles. The open invitation offered by the cutaway crotch of her flower suit has been cruelly spurned: sadly she surveys the displays of drooping members which hold out no hope for her.

The final number finishes, and Purblind and his group begin to disconnect their amplifiers and pseudo-apparatus. Strands of his shoulder-length hair stick to his sweaty neck.

All over the hired hall loin microcloths are being wrapped round sticky thighs of all dimensions, sagging breasts re-upholstered in autoheated supports and fatigued flesh put to rest in plastic codpieces. The middle-aged class has managed yet another performance. Slowly the seedy people detumesce toward the door.

In a little dressing-room, Thriply Purblind, an old youth, lifts off his wig and wipes his steaming, gleaming pate with an aphrodisia scented loincloth, memento of more virile days. He unzips his kodkorsets and gratefully allows his belly to relax in all dimensions and directions. He throws the Korsets into his travelling bag on top of the dishevelled wig before wrapping himself in his Vietnam World War Officer's Antinapalm Cape. He yawns as he carelessly drops his Multiprogrammed Miniguitar into the bag to join the other age-disguising artifacts. Wearily, he opens the dressing-room door and walks across the empty hall to the main door, which he locks, then turns off the lights and leaves the hall through the side door, which he also locks. He plods down the dark alley toward the front of the building, emerging into Pedestrian Plaza, which commemorates the famous Benny Pedestrian, the first politician to win an election on a "hugest tool" ticket.

Facing him in the Plaza is a group of the orgiasts for whom he has been playing. They are frozen into attitudes of suspicious hostility. His mean-faced rodlike patroness is standing with her legs apart and hips thrust forward, shouting in a reedy voice:

"Yer sexless quiets—there's not a man among you could even raise his member at me" as Purblind steps out of the shadowed alley into the sodium bright Plaza. The nymphos and satyrs look at him contemptuously: a sneer of frustration scars the woman's bony face.

"Impotent fat slob—huh," she snorts, tossing her head: a tear shakes loose from her brimming eyes, glistening on her sunken cheek: her blond wig slips askew, revealing a gnarled protruding ear.

"Turned off old man trying to be clever by imitating baby quiets whose balls haven't even fallen—I wouldn't allow you inside me even if you could get up."

She retracts her clean shaven pudendum and brings her feet together with a flourish.

Thriply Nasturtium Purblind halts in gobsmacked confusion. He stares at the defiant reed as she bends in the gusts of sociosexual ignominy. It occurs to him that she has not recognized him as T. N. Purblind, audio-orgiastics specialist, since he is lacking wig, corset and codpiece, and is enveloped in his black antinap cape; this in turn reminds him that he has left his bag of effects in the locked hall.

He fishes the keys from his cape pouch and turns to go back. He takes only a single pace: about a dozen figures, cowled and cloaked in black, genitals undisplayed, stand facing him in the shadows at either side of the dark alley. The Quiets: serious, autonomous, frightening youths with patient alienated eyes who observe him impartially.

An object smashes into the back of his head, hurled with all the force of frustration: it bounces and rolls across the Plaza. It is a size ten portable autopenis. It has gashed Purblind's head. Blood tickles down the back of his neck and soaks into his cape. He is dizzy. He hears a quiet voice say: "Irony; away," and half sees cowled shadows silently swallowed in fellow darkness. The patter of receding lusties behind him.

He kneels bleeding on the yielding plastic cobbles of Pedestrian Plaza, falls forward into the warm night silence, shattering it with the jangle of cascading keys, and lies dazed and dozing face downward.

Moving only toward the morning, he moans at occasional distant swishings: a street machine murmurs early cleanings in his ears, recedes, returns. Tentative antennae touch the obstructive bulk and balk. Gentle metallic sensors caress the body's contours and he clambers from an umber oblivion. Three feet before his eyes, as he now lies on his side, he sees revolving sweepers swallow the keys to his dressing-room.

In an inevitable fit of mindless altruism, the quivering mechanical menial acknowledges his existence by reporting a presence to its central automatic mentor.

Foreword to THE JUNGLE ROT KID ON THE NOD

This book is dedicated to Philip José Farmer, author of "The Jungle Rot Kid on the Nod," which is the last story in the book, but the one which started it all. When I read "Jungle Rot Kid" in manuscript, and learned that Phil Farmer couldn't find a publisher for it, I said, "Jesus Christ, Phil, someday I've got to do a book so I can publish this thing." Later, the story was published in a rather rank magazine through the intercession of some very good people, among them Brian Kirby, former editor of Essex House books, and then in New *Worlds,* so the story first saw print without my help. Nevertheless, it was the genesis of this book.

Although "Jungle Rot Kid" is a kind of pastiche, basically a funny piece, in a curious way it epitomizes Farmer as a writer and as a human being. To begin with, no one but Farmer would have thought of such a piece. I don't know anyone else who is such a dedicated *Edgar Rice* Burroughs expert and also knows who *William* Burroughs is, let alone has the ability to write exactly like him. As the incredibly diverse literary streams of the two Burroughs merge in this story, so do the traditions of the old science fiction and the new speculative fiction merge in the work of Philip José Farmer.

Farmer was the original revolutionary in the science fiction genre. His story "The Lovers," being just about the first mature and honest treatment of a sexual theme in science fiction, created a furor in the 1950s. One editor even categorically refused to consider any more stories by a man capable of writing "such filth." Nearly twenty years later, Farmer's novels for Essex House, *The Image of the Beast, A Feast Unknown,* and *Blown,* combining genuine speculative elements with uncompromising sexual realism, were similarly attacked by outraged traditionalists. In between, Farmer has written scores of novels and stories, some of them admittedly strictly commercial fiction, but the best of them adding up to a truly impressive body of work. Through periods of having to write at top speed to keep afloat; despite bouts of incredibly shoddy editorial treatment, through personal disasters that would have driven a lesser man to his knees, Farmer has continued to turn out work like "Sail On! Sail On!," "Riders of The Purple Wage," "Carats in the Head," "Lord Tiger," "Inside Outside," and "The Alley God."

Throughout his career, Farmer has been a man ahead of his time, working in a field in which most of the editors and critics were incapable of distinguishing his most meaningful work from his more mundane product. Like other talented science fiction writers of the fifties, Farmer was an idealist in a field dominated by commercially oriented cynics. But unlike many of these men who were broken and became cynical hacks themselves or fled the field they loved to save themselves, Farmer not only stood his ground and survived, but in the long run has prevailed.

Today, the best of his work is as fresh and daring as "The Lovers" was in the fifties, and stories like "Riders of the Purple Wage" and "Carats in the Head," as well as the story you are about to read, stand as proof that Farmer is more than an iconoclast, that his mastery of style can match his originality of vision.

If the whole checkered history of the evolution of commercial science fiction into modern speculative fiction has produced one genuine hero, it is Philip José Farmer, the ever-youthful granddaddy of us all.

THE JUNGLE ROT KID

ON THE NOD

by Philip José Farmer

If William Burroughs instead of Edgar Rice Burroughs
had written the Tarzan novels . . .

Foreword

*Tapes cut and respliced at random by Brachiate
Bruce, the old mainliner chimp, the Kid's asshole
buddy, cool blue in the orgone box*

from the speech in Parliament of Lord Greystoke
alias The Jungle Rot Kid, a full house, SRO, the Kid really packing them in.

—Capitalistic pricks! Don't send me no more foreign
aid! You corrupting my simple black folks, they driving
around the old plantation way down on the Zambezi
River in air-conditioned Cadillacs, shooting horse, flapping ubangi at me . . . Bwana him not in the cole cole

ground but him sure as shit gonna be soon. Them M-16s, tanks, mortars, flamethrowers coming up the jungle trail, ole Mao Charley promised us!

Lords, Ladies, Third Sex! I tole you about apeomorphine but you dont lissen! You got too much invested in the Mafia and General Motors, I say you gotta kick the money habit too. Get them green things offen your back . . . nothing to lose but your chains that is stocks, bonds, castles, Rollses, whores, soft toilet paper, connection with The Man . . . it a long long way to the jungle but it worth it, build up your muscle and character cut/

. . . you call me here at my own expense to degrade humiliate me strip me of loincloth and ancient honored title! You hate me cause you hung up on civilization and I never been hooked. You over a barrel with smog freeways TV oily beaches taxes inflation frozen dinners time-clocks carcinogens neckties all that shit. Call me noble savage . . . me tell you how it is where its at with my personal tarzanic *purushárta* . . . involves kissing off *dharma* and *artha* and getting a fix on *moksha* through *kama* . . .

Old Lord Bromley-Rimmer who wear a merkin on his bald head and got pecker and balls look like dried-up grapes on top a huge hairy cut-in fold-out thing it disgust you to see it, he grip young Lord Materfutter's crotch and say—Dearie what kinda gibberish that, Swahili, what?

Young Lord Materfutter say—Bajove, some kinda African cricket doncha know what?

. . . them fuckin Ayrabs run off with my Jane again . . . intersolar communist venusian bankers plot . . . so it back to the jungle again, hit the arboreal trail, through the middle tearass, dig Numa the lion, the lost civilizations kick, tell my troubles to Sam Tantor alias The Long Dong Kid. Old Sam alway writing amendments to the protocols of the elders of mars, dipping his trunk in the blood of innocent bystanders, writing amendments

230

in the sand with blood and no one could read what he had written there selah

Me, I'm only fuckin free man in the world . . . live in state of anarchy, up trees . . . every kid and lotsa grown-ups (so-called) dream of the Big Tree Fix, of swinging on vines, freedom, live by the knife and unwritten code of the jungle . . .

Ole Morphodite Lord Bromley-Rimmer say— Dearie, that Anarchy, that one a them new African nations what?

The Jungle Rot Kid bellowing in the House of Lords like he calling ole Sam Tantor to come running help him outta his mess, he really laying it on them blue-blood pricks.

. . . I got *satyagraha* in the ole original Sanskrit sense of course up the ass, you fat fruits. I quit. So long. Back to the Dark Continent . . . them sheiks of the desert run off with Jane again . . . blood will flow . . .

Fadeout. Lord Materfutter's face phantom of erection wheezing paregoric breath. —Dig that leopardskin jockstrap what price glory what? cut/

This here extracted from John Clayton's diary which he write in French God only know why . . . *Sacre bleu! Nom d'un con!* Alice she dead, who gonna blow me now? The kid screaming his head off, he sure don't look like gray-eyed black-haired fine-chiseled featured scion of noble British family which come over with Willie the Bastard and his squarehead-frog goons on the Anglo-Saxon Lark. No more milk for him no more ass for me, carry me back to old Norfolk // double cut

The Gorilla Thing fumbling at the lock on the door of old log cabin which John Clayton built hisself. Eyes stabbing through the window. Red as two diamonds in a catamite's ass. John Clayton, he rush out with a big axe, gonna chop me some anthropoid wood.

Big hairy paws strong as hold of pusher on old jungle whirl Clayton around. Stinking breath. Must smoke banana peels. *Whoo! Whoo!* Gorilla Express dingdonging up black tunnel of my rectum. Piles burst like rotten tomatoes, sighing softly. Death come. And come. And come. Blazing bloody orgasms. Not a bad way to go . . . but you cant touch my inviolate white soul . . . too late to make a deal with the Gorilla Thing? Give him my title, Jaguar, moated castle, ole faithful family retainer he go down on you, opera box . . . *ma tante de pisse* . . . who take care of the baby, carry on family name? *Vive la bougerie!* cut/

Twenty years later give take a couple, the Jungle Rot Kid trail the killer of Big Ape Momma what snatch him from cradle and raise him as her own with discipline security warm memory of hairy teats hot unpasteurized milk . . . the Kid swinging big on vines from tree to tree, fastern hot baboonshit through a tin horn. Ant hordes blitzkrieg him like agenbite of intwat, red insect-things which is exteriorized thoughts of the Monster Ant-Mother of the Crab Nebula in secret war to take over this small planet, this Peoria Earth.

Monkey on his back, Nkima, eat the red insect-things, wipe out trillions with flanking bowel movement, Ant-Mother close up galactic shop for the day . . .

The Kid drop his noose around the black-assed motherkiller and haul him up by the neck into the tree in front of God and local citizens which is called go-mangani in ape vernacular.

—You gone too far this time the Kid say as he core out the motherkillers asshole with fathers old hunting knife and bugger him old Turkish custom while the motherkiller rockin and rollin in death agony.

Heavy metal Congo jissom ejaculate catherinewheeling all over local gomangani, they say—Looka that!

Old junkie witch doctor coughing his lungs out in sick gray African morning, shuffling through silver dust of old kraal.

—You say my son's dead, kilt by the Kid?

Jungle drums beat like aged wino's temples morning after.

Get Whitey!

The Kid sometime known as Genocide John really liquidate them dumbshit gomangani. Sure is a shame to waste all that black gash the Kid say but it the code of the jungle. Noblesse obleege.

The locals say—We dont haffa put up with this shit and they split. The Kid dont have no fun nomore and this chimp ass mighty hairy not to mention chimp habit of crapping when having orgasm. Then along come Jane alias Baltimore Blondie, she on the lam from Rudolph Rassendale type snarling—You marry me Jane else I foreclose on your father's ass.

The Kid rescue Jane and they make the domestic scene big, go to Europe on The Civilized Caper but the Kid find out fast that the code of the jungle conflict with local ordinances. The fuzz say you cant go around putting a full-nelson on them criminals and breakin their necks even if they did assault you they got civil rights too. The Kid's picture hang on post office and police station walls everywhere, he known as Archetype Archie and by the Paris fuzz as *La Magnifique Merde*—50,000 francs dead or alive. With the heat moving in, the Kid and Baltimore Blondie cut out for the tree house.

Along come La sometime known as Sacrifice Sal elsewhere as Disembowelment Daisy. She queen of Opar, ruler of hairy little men-things of the hidden colony of ancient Atlantis, the Kid always dig the lost cities kick. So the Kid split with Jane for awhile to ball La.

—Along come them fuckin Ayrabs again and abduct Jane, gangbang her . . . she aint been worth a shit since . . . cost me all the jewels and golden ingots I heisted offa Opar to get rid of her clap, syph, yaws, crabs, pyorrhea, double-barreled dysentery, busted rectum, split urethra, torn nostrils, pierced eardrums, bruised kidneys, nymphomania, old hashish habit, and things too disgusting to mention . . .

Along come The Rumble To End All Rumbles 1914 style, and them fuckin Huns abduct Jane . . . they got preying-mantis eyes with insect lust. Black anti-orgone Horbigerian Weltanschauung, they take orders from green venusians who telepath through von Hindenburg.

—*Ja wohl!* bark Leutnant Herrlipp von Dreckfinger at his Kolonel, Bombastus von Arschangst. —Ve use die Baltimore snatch to trap der gottverdammerungt Jungle Rot Kid, dot pseudo-Aryan *Oberaffenmensch,* unt ve kill him unt den all Afrika iss ours! Drei cheers for Der Kaiser unt die Krupp Familie!

The Kid balling La again but he drop her like old junkie drop pants for a shot of horse, he track down the Hun, it the code of the jungle.

Cool blue orgone bubbles sift down from evening sky, the sinking sun a bloody kotex which spread stinking scarlet gashworms over the big dungball of Earth. Night move in like fuzz with Black Maria. Mysterious sounds of tropical wilds . . . Numa roar, wild boars grunt like they constipated, parrots with sick pukegreen feathers and yellow eyes like old goofball bum Panama 1910 cry *Rache!*

Hun blood flow, kraut necks crack like cinnamon sticks, the Kid put his foot on dead ass of slain Teuton and give the victory cry of the bull ape, it even scare the shit outta Numa King of the Beasts fadeout

The Kid and his mate live in the old tree house now . . . surohc lakcaj fo mhtyhr ot ffo kcaj* chimps, Numa roar, Sheeta the panther cough like an old junkie. Jane alias The Baltimore Bitch nag, squawk, whine about them mosquitoes tsetse flies ant-things hyenas and them uppity gomangani moved into the neighborhood, they'll turn a decent jungle into slums in three days, I aint prejudiced ya unnerstand some a my best friends are Waziris, whynt ya ever take me out to dinner, Nairobi only

---

* Old Brachiate Bruce splice in tape backward here.

234

a thousand miles away, they really swingin there for chrissakes and cut/

. . . trees chopped down for the saw mills, animals kilt off, rivers stiff stinking with dugout-sized tapewormy turds, broken gin bottles, contraceptive jelly and all them disgusting things snatches use, detergents, cigarette filters . . . and the great apes shipped off to USA zoos, they send telegram: SOUTHERN CALIFORNIA CLIMATE AND WELFARE PROGRAM SIMPLY FABULOUS STOP NO TROUBLE GETTING A FIX STOP CLOSE TO TIAJUANA STOP WHAT PRICE FREEDOM INDIVIDUALITY EXISTENTIAL PHILOSOPHY CRAP STOP

. . . Opar a tourist trap, La running the native-art made-in-Japan concession and you cant turn around without rubbing sparks off black asses.

The African drag really got the Kid down now . . . Jane's voice and the jungle noises glimmering off like a comet leaving Earth forever for the cold interstellar abysms . . .

The Kid never move a muscle staring at his big toe, thinking of nothing—wouldn't you?—not even La's diamond-studded snatch, he off the woman kick, off the everything kick, fulla horse, on the nod, lower spine ten degrees below absolute zero like he got a direct connection with The Liquid Hydrogen Man at Cape Kennedy . . .

The Kid ride with a one-way ticket on the Hegelian Express thesis antithesis synthesis, sucking in them cool blue orgone bubbles and sucking off the Eternal Absolute . . .

DRUM AND CANDLE by David St. Clair
Non-fiction: Occult   BT 50208   95¢
A first-hand account of voodoo in modern Brazil, where
the occult permeates every aspect of life. A must book
for those interested in Black Magic.

THAT SPANISH WOMAN by F. W. Kenyon
Fiction: Historical Biography   BT 50225   95¢
Biography of one of the most glamorous women ever
to have been a queen, Empress Eugenie. She used her
wit and charm to capture the emperor of France.

DRAGONS AND NIGHTMARES by Robert Bloch
Fiction: Occult   BT 40119   75¢
The most unusual collection of fantasy short stories
ever published. By the author of *Psycho*.

KILL A WICKED MAN by John Creasey
Fiction: Crime   BT 50266   95¢
A brilliant novel of crime and sex by one of the greatest
detective writers of all time. Ranks with Simenon and
Erle Stanley Gardner.

MAFIOSO by Peter McCurtin
Fiction: Mafia   BT 50259   95¢
Inside the Mafia. Brutal as an ice-pick in the spine.
This novel won a Special Award from the Mystery
Writers of America.

JOHNNY FLETCHER MYSTERY SERIES

THE LAUGHING FOX by Frank Gruber
                                       BT 50250   95¢
THE TALKING CLOCK by Frank Gruber
                                       BT 50251   95¢
THE HONEST DEALER by Frank Gruber
                                       BT 50255   95¢

Frank Gruber books are packed with action and suspense. ". . . unusually entertaining . . ."—*New York
Times*.

GUERRILLA by Jack Slade
Fiction: Western, Lassiter Series   BT 50248   75¢
Lassiter, the lanky Texan with the fast gun and the slow drawl always takes what he wants. This time he rides right into the middle of a Mexican revolution to kill a doublecrosser.

VALLEY OF SKULLS by John Benteen
Fiction: Western, Fargo Series   BT 50249   75¢
Fargo went after a solid gold cannon and a beautiful woman—in that order. There are complications, but Fargo handled it the way he always did—one step at a time.

THE SYNDICATE by Peter McCurtin
Fiction: Mafia crime   BT 50211   95¢
A powerful, ultra-violent novel by the author who won the Mystery Writers of America award for his novel MAFIOSO.

THE DUKE'S MISTRESS by F. W. Kenyon
Fiction: Historical   BT 50207   95¢
The life story of Mary Ann Clarke. She came up from the slums of London to become the mistress of Prince Frederick Augustus, son of George III.

ESCAPE ROOM by Airey Neave
Non-fiction: Spy story   BT 50221 $1.25
The true story of how Allied servicemen were spirited out of German-held territory during WWII. "Reads more like a James Bond thriller than non-fiction."—*Bestsellers*

SKIN GAME DAME by Rod Gray
Fiction: Lady from L.U.S.T. Series   BT 50214   95¢
Eve Drum, the worlds sexiest spy, swings into action in Denmark where she finds the blue movie business is a cover for some dirty intrigue.

TO KILL A KILLER by Kyle Hunt
Fiction: Mystery   BT 50231   95¢
A no-holds-barred violent murder mystery with almost unbearable suspense and tension, by the author of KILL ONCE, KILL TWICE.

THE ANALOG BULLET by Martin Smith
Fiction: Mystery   BT 50210   95¢
An exciting, complex novel with an authentic Washington D.C. background. By the author of GYPSY IN AMBER.

KILLER BOY WAS HERE by George Bagby
Fiction: Mystery   BT 50213   95¢
A blood-spattered murder mystery. The *New York Times* calls it: "Solid work, appropriate to the current mood of senseless violence."

DEATH OF THE OTHER SELF by Peter Packer
Non-fiction: Crime   BT 50206   95¢
A chiller in the tradition of Truman Capote's IN COLD BLOOD. "Highly readable"—The *New York Times*.

THE SYNDICATE by Peter McCurtin
Fiction: Mafia   BT 50211   95¢
A powerful ultra-violent novel by the Mystery Writers of America Special Award winning author of MAFIOSO.

THE ENFORCER (originally "Brain Guy")
by Benjamin Appel
Fiction: Crime   BT 50283   95¢
A savage novel wrenched from the guts of the New York underworld. ". . . a brilliant book written with the cold corroding passion of one who has seen through the heart of human poverty and degradation . . ."—*New York Times*.

GOTHIC CLASSICS

THE DUNGEON by Mary Lee Falcon
BT 50216   75¢
When Cathy inherited Stonecliff little did she know that she would soon descend into its dungeon to unleash its loathsome secret—or die.

UNHOLY SPELL by Claire Vincent
BT 50234   75¢
Emily dreamed of wedded happiness, instead, she met evil in the creaking house on the hill. Original title: "Spellbound."

ACT OF LOVE by Celia Dale   BT 50238   95¢
Evil was no stranger to Bulmer Hall. Beneath its serenity ran currents of treachery and desire. "Haunting and macabre"—*Bestsellers*.

TERROR AT DEEPCLIFF by Dorothea Nile
BT 50243   75¢
Alice knew that some dreadful secret lay buried behind the grim walls of Deepcliff, but who was so desperately anxious to keep her from uncovering it?

THE HOUSE ON SKY HIGH ROAD
by Isabel Stewart Way   BT 50252   75¢
The moment Paula stepped through the door of the old house she knew she had made a mistake. Something horrible was going on.

THE HOUSE OF DEADLY NIGHT by Iris Barry
BT 50253   75¢
Mystery and death shrouded the estate, threatening Lucinda. Was she to be the next victim? The story of a beautiful girl in deep distress.

THE DEADLY ROSE by Kathleen Rich
BT 40120   75¢
A chilling novel of a girl in flight with no place to go. Was Gaby to disappear in the night, like the others?

BELMONT TOWER BOOKS
P.O. Box 2050
Norwalk, Conn. 06852

Please send me the books listed below.

ORDER BY BOOK NUMBER ONLY.

Quantity	Book No.	Price
. . . .	. . . . . .	. . . .
. . . .	. . . . . .	. . . .
. . . .	. . . . . .	. . . .
. . . .	. . . . . .	. . . .
. . . .	. . . . . .	. . . .
. . . .	. . . . . .	. . . .

In the event we are out of stock of any of the books listed, please list alternate selections below.

. . . .	. . . . . .	. . . .
. . . .	. . . . . .	. . . .
. . . .	. . . . . .	. . . .
. . . .	. . . . . .	. . . .

I enclose $. . . . . .

Add 15¢ per book to help cover cost of postage and handling. Buy 4 or more books and we will pay the cost. Add 15¢ for every Canadian dollar order. Send cash, check or money order. No stamps.

NAME . . . .
(Please print)

ADDRESS . . . .

CITY . . . . STATE . . . . ZIP . . . .